Fire War

T. T. MICHAEL

ISBN: 1517180740
ISBN 13: 9781517180744

THE PAST

July 14th, 2051. 15.15 hours
Wrigley Field, Chicago, USA

The sun burnt down on the bleachers and Tom wriggled uncomfortably on his metal seat. He was hot, sweat trickling down the back of his neck, but he didn't want to ruin this—his first real baseball game. He didn't want to disappoint his father who hadn't wanted to take him until his mother insisted. He was worried that complaining would spoil the mood and end the afternoon, although it was sticky, loud, and sweaty. Seven, he thought to himself, was certainly old enough to be sitting up here watching one of the biggest games of the season—the Cubs versus the Giants. Both are big names, though the Cubs were going to whoop some Giant ass today; he just knew it. He glanced over at the scoreboard, smiling to himself as he read the glowing numbers. A fanfare blared so loud that he felt the music vibrate inside his chest.

"Okay, Tommy boy?" asked his father, looking down briefly and grinning at the serious look on the boy's face. Maybe he'd been wrong and Kim was right; the kid was old enough for this. The boy was doing well. He'd try to remember to pick up some flowers on the way home to make up for the yelling this morning. It could be he'd even be able to sneak in a couple of beers with the guys before they had to get back, since Tom was behaving himself so well.

"All good," Tom said, trying to ignore the prickly feeling of drying sweat in the small of his back and a mild, but increasingly growing, urge to pee. "All good," he repeated, as much to reassure himself as anyone else.

Up and down the aisles, vendors hawked peanuts, beer, and hot dogs, and people milled around, getting back to their seats for the beginning of the fourth inning. Tom's hand itched inside the big foam hand his father had bought him, emblazoned with the Cub's logo. He was more than sure that his beloved Cubs were going to win. A small breeze buzzed across the field, faintly carrying the scent of cut grass over the sweat and alcohol. Life was good.

The breeze tickled the hair on the back of his neck and Tommy sighed. It felt nice after the heat. Suddenly, it got stronger, and a rumbling, roaring sound replaced the metallic jollity of the baseball field jingles. Unconsciously, Tom slid closer to his father, who looked down, annoyed that the boy was asking for affection now, in the middle of a manly day. Kim spoiled the kid, and he reconsidered his idea of buying her flowers.

Tom felt his father stiffen so he pulled away, not wanting to be yelled at. However, the noises grew louder, and people stirred. Almost as one, they turned their heads to the sky. The sun seemed to have gone behind a cloud. Tommy wanted to look up, too, but he was afraid.

"Man up," he told himself. "Man up." It was what his father always told him, and there was nothing more that he wanted than to be a man. So he took a deep breath, filling his nose with the scents of baseball, and looked up to the sky, squinting a little.

It was a plane, not far from the blimp he had noticed earlier; that was all. Nothing to be afraid of. A tiny sigh of relief escaped his lips as he saw the familiar shape outlined over his head, wings spread out against the sky.

It was the last thing he saw before the explosion ripped his small body apart with the force of a hundred suns. The quiet of thousands of lives extinguished in the blink of a second took over, disturbed only by falling rubble. The sun beat down again, hot and sticky, on what remained of Tom, his father, and all the others who had been unfortunate enough to be at Wrigley Field for the biggest game of the season.

1

February 18th, 2076
Mexico City

Gunnery Sergeant Anthony Jackson shifted his weight almost imperceptibly from one foot to the other. It was an old trick that he'd learned on the parade grounds, one that let him stand seemingly immobile for hours at a time. He was used to this by now, and there was no chance of his making a spectacle of either himself or his president. This was a momentous occasion, after all; he wouldn't want to do anything stupid. Yet his knees ached more than a little, if he was honest. He was standing here only for the TV cameras, and he was yearning to get into position. As soon as the president got into the limo that would take him to the large stadium where the meeting was to be held, Jackson would be headed by chopper to that same stadium to take up a sniper position above the stage. Protecting his country, his president, and his people was what he did.

Standing firmly at attention, he let his mind wander off to distract him from the pain in his legs. He recited the history in his head. The NAU, or North American Union, had once been two separate countries, one called the United States and the other Canada, although he couldn't remember both names half the time. The two came together with the formation of the Union back in 2051. Back then, the United States had been a prosperous nation. After years of difficult and uncertain times, the economy had finally started improving, and the country was on the rise again. At least that was what the president of the time, President James K. Palmer, had promised. Jackson had seen the election videos and watched the debates for a paper he had written for his high school government class. He remembered the man's face quite clearly. And to be fair, the country had been doing better than it had for decades, and most of that seemed due to Palmer's leadership.

Palmer had been the kind of president that was really hands on with the economy. He made sure to do everything he could to remove unnecessary laws that were hindering the small businesses of the nation. He wanted to be sure that the people that lived in the United States were not only happy but also excited for the future. With his approach to governing and the various technological innovations and improvements in the medical field, people were living longer. Menial tasks were able to be completed by robotics improvements, leading to more free time for workers to enjoy. 'A modern-day Renaissance,' Jackson had written in his paper. The videos from that time showed a happy nation, one that he'd gladly have lived in himself.

Couple all this with a reduction in the unemployment rate, which had gone from 9.3 to 4.9 in the span of about five years, and people had more money as well to provide comfortable longer lives. There was a job for every employee. The country was practically begging for people to immigrate to take the surplus of jobs that were made available due to economic prosperity.

Crime was also down. It seemed that once the unemployment problems were fixed and most people who wanted a job had one, crimes of necessity stopped. There were drug sales and smuggling still, and not everyone wanted a clean life, but things were definitely better. They were so much better that people had started moving back to Detroit, which had been one of the most dangerous and neglected areas of the old United States.

However, while there was all this abundance in the United States, other countries were not doing nearly as well. The only country that could nearly match the level of growth and stability of the United States was Canada. Canada had been doing well because of the new oil pipeline that had been established between the countries, which allowed them to export large amounts of oil for a lower cost, which led to extremely high profits for companies and the country.

Jackson once again shifted his weight back to his right leg, this time unconsciously. His mind was lost in the history lessons of his past, following the delicate thread that had led them all to right here, right now.

While the United States was increasing in wealth and stature the world over, one of President Palmer's initiatives was to end a number of the wars that the nation had been involved in overseas. Palmer had even brought back some of the troops from various occupations in different countries, all by the end of his first term in 2048. President Palmer was the kind of guy that would keep the momentum going; the electorate were sure of it.

So sure were they, in fact, and so high were Palmer's popularity ratings, that he was reelected by the second largest margin in American history. He showed his gratitude to the voters by rewarding them with lower tax rates and bringing even more new jobs to the country. People dubbed this era the 'Roaring Fifties', but all that would not last for long. Eventually the good times had to end. It is human nature to worry and be cautious. Those who paid attention in their history classes knew how the roaring twenties ended over a hundred years ago – with the crash and Great Depression, causing desperation until war rolled around to improve the economy once again. Meanwhile, over in Canada things were going equally well. Canada remained a first-world country and had been experiencing a boom of her own after the installation of the joint U.S.-Canadian oil pipeline. In truth, Canada was making so much money that even the government was having trouble spending it all. Nationalized healthcare was expanded, allowing even cosmetic services like liposuction and face remodeling to citizens for a small deductible price. High school graduates were given two years of free post-grad education, ensuring that the country would continue to move forward and progress both technologically and socially.

Furthermore, the state of relations between the U.S. and Canada was closer than ever before. For the first time in their histories, both countries were dependent on each other, and this worked surprisingly well. Mutual dependence led to financial success, to happiness, and to peace.

July 14th, 2051—the day the world came crashing down. At 3:15 P.M., bombs simultaneously exploded in four major areas of the United States and Canada. A further attack against New York was thwarted, the city having been on high alert and cautious since the bombings of 2001.

In Chicago, people were settling themselves down into their seats to watch the fourth inning of the Giants versus Cubs game when their world exploded into a fiery ball of flames and flying debris. At first, those watching the game on TV thought there was some kind of half-time show—some pyrotechnic display perhaps.

The signal cut out and then showed the stadium from above. Viewers thought that the network had made a mistake—that the station must have stuck in a tape of an old disaster movie. The station then cut out completely as they realized what they were broadcasting.

At the same time in Canada, the CN Tower came toppling down. First-on-the-scene reports put it down to structural failure, but their cameras had been too slow to capture the collapse itself. Blaming a long dead architect was easy. But, within an hour, a YouTuber by the name of EZMap343 uploaded a video he'd taken of the event to Reddit. The video rapidly went viral, showing the world that only an explosion could have caused the damage. This revelation led to the evacuation of all CN Towers globally, as well as most skyscrapers. However, the information came too late to save the Willis Tower in downtown Chicago. It came tumbling to the ground in pieces, killing nearly everyone inside and those within radius of the falling metal and glass. Many of the entryways to Union Station were blocked and the fragments of buildings nearly kept the river from flowing. Every reporter referred to the building by its old and more familiar name of the Sears Tower in this time of crisis.

Toronto's Rogers Stadium was hosting a down-to-the-wire Blue Jays game. Folks sat on the edges of their seats, roaring in joy or disappointment, thinking about the important things like if they should have another corndog or beer, or whether or not the Jays could really pull this off, and then they were gone. The idle thoughts of breathing, living beings, ball players and spectators, coaches and hot dog vendors, all gone in a hot, loud explosion of pure power.

For some, these were signs that the Apocalypse had come. This was the end of days; Christ would rise again and bring them all to rapture in the sky. Jackson had to stop himself, smiling a little in derision, reminding himself to keep a straight face. There were always people like that, no matter what happened in the world, although these turned out to be more important than many; the media dubbed them Apocalytes. In the months following the explosions, they were nothing but a mere nuisance with their calls to repentance. As the likelihood of the rapture coming faded, they became enemies of the State, though those days were still in the future in 2051. Still, though, there were always those looking for the comfort of salvation when, of course, the solution was far more banal and a lot more human.

Rumors spread faster than wildfire—Al Qaeda. But how could they, in their diminished state, have organized and planned something so big? It had been almost fifty years since the World Trade Center bombings of 2001. Al Qaeda no longer had the force, the power, or the supporters to do this. Not that that stopped the press from blaming them. Or maybe it was ISIS? The Syrian-based terror organization had gone from strength to strength, terrifying not just Middle Eastern nations, but a fair few European countries as well. Had they finally set their sights on North America?

All of this was pure speculation, though it gave the news stations hours of programming to entertain the masses. It wasn't until a DVD disc was sent to the New York City offices of NBC that anyone found out what was really going on. The FBI forbade the airing of the video, but in a rare show of better judgment, the station played it anyway just hours after the FBI said not to. That is when the world heard the name 'Hariq Jihad' for the first time.

Hariq Jihad, or Fire War in translation, claimed full responsibility for the bombing, though they gave no real reason for the destruction. They simply promised to wage war on North America and to plunge the continent back into the Stone Age. The United

States and Canada were going to have to be more than vigilant after this.

In the days following the attacks of July 14th, people rushed to judgment. One thing was certain: no one wanted to live their lives in fear, and most were willing to do whatever was necessary to get the government to stem the influx of Hariq Jihad supporters. This war, it was argued, needed to be finished before it really started; these people could not be allowed to take a decent and God-fearing country. The people of North America would not be brought to their knees. Pundits and talk show hosts preached the necessity of change: the country had to change, the government had to change, and the people had to change. Those in power knew that they had no choice—that the changes had to be made before the people turned on them; that control had to be kept in order to stop people taking matters into their own hands.

Meanwhile there were protests and riots in the streets, reminding those old enough to remember of the Watts riots in the 1960s. Power slowly slid out of the hands of law officials and governors, and no one knew how to stop it. Congress was stumped, no closer to resolution, while the American people called on their country to take care of them. On July 27th, a transformer blew in Los Angeles, taking down the electrical grid for the entire Western seaboard for over a week. It was unclear whether this was an accident or deliberate tampering, but it mattered little. These were rough days for the country.

Residents cried out for the restoration of sanity and peace, so the governors of the west coast states collectively decided to bring in martial law. Curfews were enacted and looting stopped dead in its tracks. FEMA was called in and band aids were applied across the most urgent wounds and issues.

This was far from enough, though. The citizens of the United States and Canada begged for their countries to be made safer, for assurances that this could never happen again. They called out for new laws to be made, new treaties to be forged, new rulers to be elected. But they were unaware of the true consequences of what they were demanding.

It was, Jackson mused, tensing and releasing his shoulder muscles to ease his stiffness, a dilemma. Did the people push the government into making draconian law, or did the government want to do so anyway and let the people think it was their idea? And did it really matter? By the time it became apparent what was happening, those who tried to apply the brakes found that it was far too late to change the direction of things—that tides couldn't be turned.

Within months, laws for stability were passed by both countries, but rioting had gotten out of control in the weeks following the attacks. The United States, which had been a nation brought together by the tragic events of September 11th, 2001, now saw a country torn apart at the seams fifty years later. The economy hit a nose dive, and as security and comfort leaked away, so too did jobs, money, and luxuries.

With Canada so dependent on the U.S. economy, her stock markets plunged and in the end there was only one answer. Canada was bailed out by the United States, unable to support herself and pay off her debts. The U.S. came to her aid, but with a proviso: together the two countries would pursue a new agreement to form one country under two presidents to be known as the North American Union. And so, with an act of congress signed by the President of the United States and the Prime Minister of Canada, upheld by the Supreme Courts of both countries, the NAU was born. With a combined economy and fighting forces, both countries' civilian populations felt more at ease, and after all, this hadn't been a big step. The past decade had seen the two countries grow close. The NAU seemed a natural progression.

Then came the constitutional amendments. Mostly, the laws of the NAU were based on those of the original United States, and since ten ex-Canadian states had been added to the confederation, a continental congress had to be called. Some called for the ratification and reaffirmation of the original US Constitution and Bill of Rights, but others demanded further protections from the enemy. So the constitution was changed to reflect a more modern age.

This came as a great disappointment to the Apocalytes, who were already growing in number. They believed that the horrors of the last few months, not to mention many of the coming problems that the NAU would face, were caused by the abandonment of the original constitution. Their numbers were made up of individuals from different walks of life and backgrounds, although many of the organizers had had some involvement with the Libertarian party before the attacks. They centered their beliefs on the principles of the original founding fathers; ignoring the wisdom and laws set forth by them would lead to the world being punished for this mistake. But so far, a man could believe what he wished as freedom of speech hadn't yet been revoked, so the little cult grew and the rest of the population did what they could to ignore them.

It had been a long road, Jackson thought—a very long road. With a flicker of his eye, he saw President Meyers of the NAU hold out a hand to the Mexican President Espinoza and shake firmly, smiling genuinely as he did so. Suddenly, Jackson's legs felt less tired and he straightened up a little bit, just enough to show a little respect. His journey had been a long one, too; it was no wonder that his legs ached after walking such a long road...

2

THE TRAINING

A Month Earlier: January 11ᵗʰ, 2076
Somewhere in Mexico

Anthony Jackson was tall and slender. He was right-handed, yet held his weapon in his left, something that he was certain had helped him become the excellent marksman he was today. With his meager start in a white trash farm house with barely enough food to keep his belly full, he had never expected to become one of the best snipers in the NAU Forces.

He was almost six feet tall, something he knew from days when he would be a decoy in the local police line-ups. This was back when he was still struggling to make money and desperately needed to buy a fancy ring to propose to his girlfriend.

He was built like a house, with muscles rippling under every surface of skin. His muscles bulged beneath his clothes, making his clothes fit tight. He worked out every day, sometimes more than once. Some thought it was his military training that drove his regimen, but he knew it was because he missed his wife and girls so much when he was on duty that it physically hurt him. The repetition of constantly lifting and curling and running helped keep his mind focused on what was in front of him.

He'd been lucky: that beautiful girlfriend had accepted the beautiful ring, once he'd scraped up enough cash to buy it, and agreed to marry him. He had never been happier, or at least he thought so. However, once he'd seen the 3D ultrasound of his oldest daughter in utero—her calm little presence, her delicate arms—only then had he realized that he had space for more joy. Two and a half years later, another daughter joined them. They were ten and seven years old now, and he missed them, more than he had ever thought possible.

All he wanted was to finish up this last engagement and settle down to become a family man. It was all he'd ever wanted. He spent all the time he possibly could with them when he wasn't posted or on duty, but that wasn't the kind of time he wanted them to have. It was a time when he was torn between his love for them and the horror of having to leave them behind again in hours, days, or weeks to go back to the battlefield. This reality made him distant, colder than he should have been when he was around them. It was like he didn't want to get too attached to them because, at any moment, he could be called away to fight against the Hariq Jihad. It wasn't selfishness—it was protection for both parties. He didn't want his girls getting too close because he could die any day, and he didn't want to tear out their hearts. If he stayed cold, maybe they'd love him less fiercely, but maybe it wouldn't hurt so much if he didn't come home one day.

This was all going to change when he retired. He'd be the kind of dad he'd always wanted to be—the dad that grilled outside in the yard, that helped with homework, and that went to piano recitals. In his heart, all he'd ever wanted was to be a father, a real father, like the ones that you saw on old TV shows from the twentieth century. Forget riches and travelling and seeing the world—Jackson's dreams were far simpler than that. The world could see to itself, and he'd be happy never to leave the NAU again once his tour ended.

He chuckled to himself as he stretched out his long body on the military issue bunk, feeling the bed creak under him as his muscles tensed up and then relaxed. A ceiling fan turned leisurely on the ceiling, creaking slightly, though there was no other noise. It was early, too early even for Jackson to be up, but awake he was and with good reason. Today was the day that he got started on the journey towards achieving his wish. After years of fighting and sweating and shooting, he could finally see the light at the end of the tunnel.

Bed springs bounced as he rolled over, the pillowcase scratchy on his cheek, but the window was still dark with no sign of dawn just yet. The Marine Corp. had sent him down here to God-knows-where, Mexico to train Mexican soldiers in the fine art of marksmanship so they too could be great snipers, like him. He knew that he was going to be making a difference here, as he had seen the slovenly ways of the soldiers he was going to train. Oh yes, he'd have them in tip-top condition in no time, and then he'd be free. According to his commanding officer, this was his last engagement. He would return home to his wife and kids, and be normal again. He had no intention of making the forces his career, he was going to be a civilian, and a good one at that.

Never again would he have to fight for his life, be scared, and think about how badly things worked. He wouldn't need to keep the tragedies of war to himself—to keep secrets from his wife and kids because he didn't want them to feel his pain, his fear.

A slim sliver of gray appeared in the middle of the window, finally a chance of some light. Jackson sat up, stretching again. He wanted to daydream a little more of all the things that he'd do at home—all he'd have and all he'd give to his girls, but he needed to get into a work mindset, focusing on the task at hand. He pushed the girls to the back of his mind. He was going to think about war now, going to think about being the best sniper he could be and teaching these men how to be the best snipers that they could be. Little did they all know that being a sniper, being a good sniper, meant living in trees for days at a time while you waited to get your shot. Jackson gave a grim smile, this was going to be the final thing that he taught them, and they were going to hate him for it, but he was glad to do it because it would mean that it was almost time to go home.

As he jumped out of bed, he was already standing in front of the grimy mirror. He grabbed his flimsy military razor and scraped at his whiskers. He was interrupted by a knock on the door.

"Wake up call, sir!" came the voice from outside.

"Received," said Jackson without even thinking about it, so used to receiving and acknowledging such messages. It had taken his wife two months to figure out that the only way to reliably get him out of bed in the morning was to issue a military style "wake up call."

Face as smooth as it was going to get, Jackson turned to his limited wardrobe and considered his choices. After a moment's reflection, he bypassed the special sniper gear that he'd usually wear out in the brush and put on his camos instead. He was in Mexico; he figured he could dress down a little and get away with the more comfortable camouflage gear. Nodding at himself in the mirror, satisfied that he looked neat enough to inspire respect and large enough to inspire fear, he prepared to leave his quarters. The men had been issued the same wakeup call as he had, and if they were anything close to smart, they'd make sure that they beat him to the briefing room that he'd reserved for the morning.

Purposefully, he trotted down the corridor, mind intent on what he was about to do. He reached the room he needed and put his hand on the door handle, twisting a little. He paused, enjoying the power trip of the sound of a dozen or so chairs pushed back and men scrambling to attention before they even saw who was coming. Throwing the door open, he strode in.

"At ease!" he barked in his booming voice. "Names and ranks."

In quick succession, the men sounded off their personal information, and, not for the first time, Jackson was glad that nearly everyone in Mexico had become fluent in English, mostly due to the large NAU presence in the country. The days when you couldn't find a guy who'd understand you wanted a bottle of non-deadly and preferably NAU-issued water were long gone. Everyone spoke English these days, even the damn terrorists. In fact, that was one of their grievances. In the last twenty-five years or so, things had skewed so much towards the NAU and its huge superpower status that it made things difficult for people in other countries to retain their culture. Not that it mattered all that much to Jackson; there was no stopping progress, he figured. He realized that he'd spaced out and hadn't really been listening to anything that the men lined up in front of him had been saying. So much for staying focused on the job.

There were fourteen of them. He allowed his eyes to run up and down their ranks, seeing hardened soldiers, but green snipers. Knowing how to fight didn't equal knowing how to shoot, and he knew that better than anyone. No one wanted to depend on a man to cover you when he couldn't hit the side of a barn with his rifle.

Five of these men were going to be chosen for a classified mission to begin in six months' time, and it was his job to have them ready to shoot. Not that Jackson knew what the mission was; it was on a need to know basis and apparently he didn't need to know. He'd find out eventually, he guessed. But in the meantime, he was to train these guys for war.

"Name and rank, repeat!" he barked, giving himself a little more time to look them over. No one balked at the order as they were all too used to doing exactly what they were told when they were told to do it.

Jackson knew that he was considered the best marksman in the Western hemisphere, so it wasn't tough to figure out that he was going to be training these guys for something special. General sniper training, sure, that was on the curriculum, but there was going to be more to it than that. He hoped, for once, that it would be something that would help people, but it wasn't like he was given a say in the decision making process. Presumably he was going to train them for some kind of mission involving Hariq Jihad, but who knew?

What felt like a lifetime of briefings as well as a keen nose for the truth behind the news reports told Jackson that the Mexican borders weren't as safe as some would have the world believe. Time and again insurgents and even fully fledged Hariq Jihad members were caught attempting to cross into or out of Mexico. This may have been because it was safer to enter the NAU by land than it was to go by sea and enter through the north, but also, Jackson felt, it was for more personal reasons.

After the Iraq wars of the early 2000's ended, many Islamic people moved away from the destruction of their country and the implications that being an Iraqi carried at the time. Many made their way to Guatemala, looking for a fresh start—a new place, a new climate. Some even changed their name to begin again, without the stigma that being an Islamic Iraqi carried. No one really knew why the migrants chose Guatemala, rather than other more hospitable countries such as Iceland, but what mattered in the end was that the Islamic community made huge inroads in the small country. The 2070 census showed Guatemala to be only slightly less than half Muslim.

Regardless of all this, what remained was the fact that Jackson, through briefings or eavesdropping or pure guesswork, heard more and more about Hariq Jihadists being caught at the Mexico-NAU border. While so far no one, as far as they knew, had managed to get into the country, it wouldn't be long before someone did, and that couldn't be allowed to happen. In the last year, Jackson had heard at least twelve believable reports of insurgents trying to cross the border, more than had been seen in decades. And that was worrying, very worrying, especially to those sworn to defend and protect the NAU. Terrorists, Jackson thought to himself wryly, suck—big time.

The men were almost done with their second roll call, and despite thinking about the job ahead, Jackson had actually managed to keep somewhat on top of names this time.

The last in the line hesitated for a moment when it came to his turn, then said, "Armani Vasquez, sir."

He sounded slightly unsure of himself, a little quieter than the other men perhaps, and Jackson immediately liked him. Vasquez reminded him of himself when he had first started the sniper program, uncertain of himself. He had been excited, hoping that the training would go well for him, but knowing that more than fifty percent of the men in the ranks with him would fail out. He had been concerned that he would be among the failures so had to find something that was going to make him stand out.

Jackson took a deep breath, surveying the men in front of him. "First," he began, "I want to say that I am Gunnery

Sergeant Anthony Jackson." He moderated his voice to make himself seem gentler than he really was. He wanted the men to fear and respect him, but he also needed to know that they would come to him with their problems, even betray secrets to him. That was important when you commanded men who you might one day rely on.

"I believe in two things: shooting well and dedication—dedication to faith, family and country. If you do not believe in these two things, then I suggest that you leave now. I will not be training anyone who doesn't want to be a part of those two essentials. Without shooting well, you can't protect your faith, family or country, and without faith, family and country, you won't be able to do what you have to do out there when you've got to shoot well. You've got to have something that you're trying to come back to. If you don't, you'll be lost, and I don't train lost men."

He stopped and looked at them, giving them time to take all this in, to understand it and take it to heart. He was serious that they had every opportunity to walk out of the room and then leave the training right now. Compared to him, these men were boys, but they needed to grow up and grow up fast. What they were going to be trained to do was one of the most stressful and terrible jobs in the forces: to be able to look at a man's face and deliberately and coldly shoot him. It was necessary, but difficult nonetheless.

"Training will be hard," he went on, after a few moments of silence. "It will be an arduous task. In six months, I expect you to know everything you can possibly know about your options for weapons, how to follow a target, and how to keep yourself alive while waiting to hit your target."

Jackson saw the hint of a smile on the face of the man in the front row.

"Smile if you want, soldier, but all the sharp shooting in the world won't make a difference if you're not able to keep yourself alive long enough to take a shot."

The man dropped his eyes to the ground.

"Now, I don't know where you guys will end up. Maybe you'll move to protecting your president, maybe you'll move on to doing something else. Maybe they'll send you off to the battlefield. But there is no doubt in my mind that you need to understand what exactly you are doing to ensure that you are going to make a difference in this world. Understanding that and yourselves will help you to become better soldiers, better marksman and the best snipers."

Once the motivational speech was over, he made sure to make eye contact with each and every one of the men under his command and then gave a sharp nod.

"Now, let's go see how you shoot."

The men let out a rousing cheer and began to troop out of the room towards the range. Jackson grinned; this was what he really wanted to see. He wanted his men to go out there and shoot, partly to see what they could already do, and because he needed to know their skill level and who had a natural affinity for shooting and who didn't. It was also because shooting stuff was a fun way to spend the day and would get them all hyped up and bonded.

■ ■ ■

For the first four weeks, as he had planned, they headed out to shoot, each day moving the targets further and further away. He'd been able to see their abilities, to point out mistakes, and correct their form. Then, the time had come for a final step—a test of their skills in a simulated experience. They were to have war games, essentially a paint ball game of sorts where they would each attempt to kill or mark a high level target from the other team. He broke the team up first into fours, then into pairs, and the pairs with the highest kill score after their five day outing in the woods would be the ones that moved on to the next level of training. For the sake of the exercise, Jackson pulled in a few new recruits to act as high-interest targets for his men.

"So," Jackson began, "this is how we'll proceed. You have twenty-four hours to secure your location within the site we've practiced at, at which time I will let off this blow horn." He deliberately pressed the button, letting them familiarize themselves with the sound and laughing internally as they all tried not to let on that the shrieking was tearing their ear drums apart. When he had drummed up enough sympathy for them, he let the horn go quiet. "As you can hear, it's a loud enough sound, so it should alert your team that the game has begun. However, should there be any question as to when the game starts, then officially it begins at 0400 hours. There will be no cheating. If you are not in the direct vicinity of your base at the start of the game, you will be disqualified, and by that, I mean the team will be disqualified. Do you understand me?"

"Sir, yes sir!"

The men, assembled in full gear, looked to be burning up under the hot sun, and Jackson didn't envy them—nor did he pity them: life was hard; they'd get used to it.

"The first to kill, and by kill, I mean tag with paint, not actually make someone devoid of life, is the winner of that particular round. Clear?"

"Sir, yes sir!" said his men again.

"Targets," he said, turning around to the two new recruits, Private Arturo and Private Sanchez, who were both from the same small town near Tijuana. A common joke on the base was that they were secretly brothers, but there was no truth to that. In fact, they had barely known each other before fate had brought them into the armed forces at the same location at that time.

"Targets, you'll be living with your men like normal, and you are to act as though you don't know that you are being hunted. They are looking to hunt you down, but don't be cowards and try and hide in a closet. Eventually, your sniper will get you, if they are a good sniper. Act cowardly and I'll make sure that you're on toilet cleaning duty for the rest of your assigned time here on this base, understood?"

The two men didn't even look at each other as they both anxiously said, "Sir, yes sir!"

"After your team of four has won or lost, you will go through this same situation again with teams of two. Privates Sanchez and Arturo, you will not have to worry about the problems of having to go through this same challenge ad nauseum. This challenge will be done once one of you is shot. We will choose another pair to assist us with the second leg of this challenge."

Jackson eyed them all one more time. The woods behind them was scrub land—very hot, dusty, and with little in the way of real foliage cover. They'd be relying on rocks, hastily dug holes and pure luck to keep themselves out of sight. No, he thought, he really didn't envy them at all. But then, these were the conditions, so they were going to have to learn how to deal with them.

"Go!" he barked.

The men took off at a run, boots sending up clouds of dust. Watching them leave, Jackson wondered who would be the first to make a kill. He had his suspicions; he'd watched all the men closely, but it would be nice to have his intuitions confirmed.

■ ■ ■

There was a rumor going around the military base that the presidents of the NAU and Mexico were going to have a face-to-face meeting. The rumor had been spreading for a while now, and was quickly becoming the only thing that anyone could talk about.

"I'm sure I'm going to be chosen," Private Daniels said, spearing a piece of potato and cramming it into his mouth. He wasn't arrogant, simply sure of himself, confident, and maybe a bit cocky, yet popular too.

"It's just a rumor," said Vasquez, picking at his mess tray, trying to find something that looked faintly edible. He had been spoiled by his mother's home cooking and the mess food was not anywhere near as edible. "The president isn't about to pick any of us for personal security detail," he added.

"I'm sure that's not true," said Daniels, through a mouth still half full of potatoes. "They just don't want us to realize that we're going to be picked for President Espinoza's secret police service, that's all."

Vasquez rolled his eyes. "And why exactly would they send one of those NAU soldiers over here to teach us how to protect our own president?" he asked. "That's ridiculous, and, well, illogical. If we were supposed to protect Espinoza against an attack when he's meeting the NAU president, then they'd hardly send NAU sniper supreme Jackson to show us how, would they?"

"Just you wait and see," Daniels said, confidently. "They're going to combine our country with theirs and create one huge mega country, just you wait."

Vasquez rolled his eyes again. "Daniels, you really need to stop listening to those conspiracy theory news shows. They're gonna get you into trouble one day."

"I'm telling you, it's gonna happen," he said.

"Right," said Vasquez. "And I'm a terrorist."

Just as their verbal disagreement was heading towards a real argument, Jackson entered the mess hall. He was clutching a cup of coffee in his hand and looking around the room for someone. His eyes finally settled on the table where Private Daniels and Sergeant Vasquez were sitting. It didn't matter, since he was looking for both of them. He watched their angry gestures as Daniels picked up a piece of potato and threw it at his comrade. Jackson realized he might regret his decision, but he simply sighed. Men would be men.

Contrary to the others' feelings, who had far less experience of mess hall food than Jackson did, he was pleased to note that the day's meal actually looked quite palatable. Well, palatable might be stretching it, but at least everything was a vaguely natural color and some of it even looked like food. The kitchens must be making an effort due to their fancy visitors, Jackson thought. Because today wasn't just any day; today they were celebrating the visit of NAU president Frederick J. Meyers, along with the vice presidents of both Mexico and the NAU. This wasn't common for a Mexican army base, but Jackson was sure that there was more than simple tourism involved.

All around him, men yelled and shouted, some in their native Spanish, though most even here were speaking English. In all stages of training, these men—these boys—would end up being sent out into the world to defend their country. And down here, most of the soldiers trained on base would be deployed out into the field to help the Mexican authorities combat the various cartels that had taken over the southern cities and provinces of Mexico. Over the last sixty years, the increasing tension between the government and the cartels had become a war in all but name.

In fact, one of the many reasons for the NAU president's trip to Mexico was to discuss how the North American Union could help the embattled country with the situation occurring on their southern border. The people of Mexico were growing restless and were beginning to demand that the government do something about the increasingly violent cartels, wanting their standards of living raised so that they no longer had to live in fear of thugs, pay protection money, worry about their children being kidnapped for ransom. Whether they liked it or not, the Mexican government knew that they needed help.

When Jackson had first been given the objectives for his mission—to work with the Mexican soldiers—he had originally been told that he would be training them to be exemplary snipers in order to aid the fight against the cartels. He had accepted it as a possibility. After the beginning of the Fire War, the Hariq Jihad had seemed to creep into every corner, destroying peaceful nations, luring even the most sedate of countries into war, whether directly or indirectly through methods like the cartels.

Jackson knew that if this were true, then he was undertaking something very risky indeed. Training a squad of men to assist in taking out high level targets in the Mexican cartels was dangerous, and he was almost certainly putting himself and maybe even his family in danger. This was particularly true since it was accepted as fact that the cartels were in cahoots with the Hariq Jihad. There had to be someone pulling the strings because the cartels kept coming out on top, even against well trained troops. The cartels scared people—not just civilians, but the government as well. They were more powerful than they had any right to be, and certainly more powerful than they deserved to be. They were simply terrorists flying a different flag, and Jackson was sure that if you took a close look at that flag, you'd see the Hariq Jihad emblem burning underneath.

The war games had been a huge success, confirming Jackson's suspicions, and making him feel more comfortable with his decision. Now that they were over, the time had come to start a new program—one that would choose only the best of the best, identifying the commanding officer of the group. This person would lead these men in the ongoing war against the military cartel members.

He had weighed many different factors in making his final decision. As he'd suspected, the winners of the war games competition were Armani Vasquez and Mike Daniels. A suspiciously NAU name, though both of Daniels's parents were Mexican. Jackson needed to choose between them.

Armani was the better shot, though not by much. However, Daniels had the necessary leadership skills to deal with any emergencies that may happen while the team was out in the thick of things. He'd be able to figure out how to solve problems that would almost certainly occur, to smooth things over, and to think with a level head. And in the end, that had been what decided the matter for Jackson. He knew that with the cartels you could never count on them acting in any specific way. They were known for their erratic behavior, either because they were a little too enthusiastic about using their own products, or because they were simply insanely paranoid due to their list of enemies.

Though watching the two men flinging pieces of food at each other across the mess hall, Jackson wondered why he'd considered either of them. He smiled a little. In truth, the decision had made him a little sad. He liked Vasquez and felt a sympathy with him that was increased when he'd walked into the bunk room a couple of weeks ago to find the other men hugging Vasquez and slapping him on the back.

"Vasquez's girl has given him a daughter!" one of the other men had told him, and Jackson had grinned and waited his turn to shake the man's hand.

"Congratulations," he'd said, and for a moment he and Vasquez had looked each other in the eye, father to father, and understood. That look said they both understood the fear of the responsibility that they'd been given—that the price paid for such a valuable gift was constant, unrelenting fear. A smile crept across Vasquez's face, which Jackson returned. He left the men to their celebration.

The afternoon before the food fight, Jackson pulled on a fresh uniform and readied to leave his quarters. The time had come to report to his commanding officer who he had chosen. He was stopped by a knock on his door.

"Enter!" he said, somewhat sharply; he was anxious to report that he'd decided who was best suited to lead the offensive against the cartels.

When his commanding officer walked into the room, Jackson could have bitten his tongue at his previous tone. Quickly he saluted.

"At ease, Jackson."

"Sir, yes sir."

The officer let his eyes roam around the room, but Jackson knew that he'd find nothing out of place and nothing to be written up for. Even without expecting an inspection, neatness was such a habit to him that he never allowed his quarters to become untidy.

"Jackson," said Commanding Officer Grimaldi, pursing his lips and looking almost disappointed that the room was so immaculate, "President Meyers is going to need a detail of snipers, one from our side and one from the Mexican forces, to guard himself and President Espinoza at a historic and extremely sensitive meeting that will happen at the end of this month."

So, thought Jackson, the rumors had been correct, but he said nothing.

"We'd like you and your best sniper to be on that team." Grimaldi frowned. "Who's the best sniper that you have in the Mexican team you've been training?"

Jackson didn't hesitate. "Hands down, it is Armani Vasquez." He was confident in this. As long as Vasquez wasn't in the thick of things, he would be the best person for the job. It was only in situations where numerous decisions needed to be made on the fly that Jackson was less confident in his abilities. As a shooter though, Vasquez was a natural, with grace, focus and an efficient, calm style. He was also a great guy, though he made a better follower than a leader.

"Why him?"

"He's a good soldier and he's the best shot they have," replied Jackson immediately.

"Good," said Grimaldi, with a brisk nod. "Have him report to my tent at 0700 hours tomorrow."

"Sir, yes sir," said Jackson, with another salute, but Grimaldi was already halfway out the door.

All of which brought Jackson to the mess hall that evening, and with a shake of his head, he strode through the crowd, eager to tell his men that a final decision had been made. He was secretly happy to be able to compensate Vasquez with an opportunity that could very well make his career.

■ ■ ■

At 0700 hours the next morning, Armani Vasquez entered Grimaldi's quarters. Jackson didn't see him again for two weeks. He assumed, when he thought about it, that Vasquez was probably undergoing tests and security clearance protocols, possibly with some leave to get his affairs in order. It didn't worry him too much; he looked forward to working with Vasquez on his return. And in the meantime, Jackson was far too busy getting the other men prepared to go out into the field to deal with the cartels. When he did spare a thought for anything that wasn't his job, it was only to say a silent goodnight in his mind to his two little girls.

3

THE MEETING

February 18th, 2076
Chicago, NAU
Article Originally Published in the *Tribune Web*, Reused with Permission

Can Meyers Woo Mexico? Or Has He Lost the Touch?
Jack Langthorpe, Political Correspondent

On February 17th, President Meyers presided over a Chicago President's Day Celebration, making him the first president to do so since Marvin Henry in 2056. This was sure to be a welcome break for the president after two weeks spent at the economic policy summit in Greece, a far from glorious occasion for the usually confident leader.

Though once well regarded, Greece has proven unable to regain her former glory after the economic collapse of late 2016; and with the rise of the Golden Dawn party as well as a major resurgence in fascist political thought in the region, the country has been unable to strengthen her economy to pre-2008 levels.

The economic summit, which began on February 3rd and was initiated by the NAU, was set to discuss what help, if any, the superpower would give the country to help her out of the latest of her current financial challenges. However, the citizens of Greece have protested any and all suggestions that the group has so far put to the Greek government.

Among rejected proposals were pension reforms and requests for the country to return to free market capitalism, a particular sticking point for President Meyers, as well as suggestions that the country reconsider her fascist government.

President Abiron Karakis of the nation's most popular Golden Dawn party is widely loved by the Greek people, having been popular since he came to power ten years prior in a landslide election against the conservative party of the country. Readers might remember the monumental election in which Karakis won eighty percent of the vote against his opponent, Christos Demetrius.

Following the monumental loss, Demetrius was later found hanging from a beam in the closet of his home in suburban Athens, in an apparent suicide. Police speculate it was due to the crushing defeat while his family continues to suspect foul play.

Due to the sudden and unexpected death of Demetrius, President Karakis' approval numbers declined significantly. In an effort to combat this, he declared a national holiday dedicated to the memory of all those Greeks that had been lost in the terrorist attacks of 2075. Official numbers are in dispute; however, the accepted count of the deceased is 4,528 including men, women, and children.

The economic summit, which focused on fixing Greece's economic woes, also looked more broadly to determine ways to deal with the continuing European depression. Members of the Euro block of countries have posted declining GDP numbers for the past three years. There has been hesitation to call it a depression; however, economists have been very explicit in their concerns.

Some critics have questioned if the recent rise of nationalism, extremism, and isolationist policies are a direct result of the economic problems that the European nations are facing. The only country that has managed to avoid much of the depression economy is Germany. German Chancellor Angela Bachmeier has credited her country's conservative economic policy, return to the gold standard, and departure from the Euro currency system as three of the many reasons why the country remains unscathed by the desperate economic climate. Other critics, however, have suggested that Germany's continued success had much to do with their long-standing trade agreement with the NAU.

While no resolution was made during the summit, President Meyers stated that he had hopes that his other political trips would be much more successful. This was an allusion to his upcoming trip to Mexico City, Mexico to meet with Mexican President Espinoza. While the entirety of the president's itinerary has yet to be released, top political analysts have speculated that the trip is to discuss admitting Mexico to the NAU and forming a stronger, more diverse nation.

Citizens of the North American Union are divided on the issue, with up to forty percent of residents opposed to the move. Five percent of people polled were undecided.

Should President Meyers be on a diplomatic mission to bring Mexico into the Union, there would be a number of far reaching consequences, considering that the Mexican government has been at war with the cartels for the past year on its southern border. But the real question that remains is whether or not the president is able to convince both the government of Mexico and his own people that the move would be wise. Given his failure to persuade the Greek government to take even elementary financial precautions, it would appear that luck will be siding with the president's detractors.

February 18th, 2076
Mexico City

Jackson put down his tablet in disgust, wishing that the story was printed like the old days, where it could be crinkled to join a letter that he'd received when he came in late the previous evening. He wasn't sure what bothered him most: that the Mexicans might be joining the Union, or that the conspiracy theorists had been right. What he did know was that he hated reading politics over breakfast. He was supposed to be calming himself down, not stressing himself out, but his eye had been caught by the words 'Mexico City,' and before he'd known it, he'd been reading through the story while simultaneously trying to scoop up scrambled eggs. He couldn't wait to be the hell out of here. Let the big boys make the big decision; he wanted out, back home, where his toughest decision all day would be whether or not to put on pants.

He stood and stretched, seeing the black uniform hanging on the back of his door. He had time; he always made sure he had time before something big like this. A great shooter was only great when he had a clear mind, as he'd been trying to teach his men. Although they'd sneered at his suggestion, Jackson was more than confident that meditation was all that stood between success and failure, at least for him. Vasquez had seemed to take the idea seriously, and that gave Jackson a little hope and a lot of confidence in his soon to be colleague.

Lowering himself to the floor, curling in his legs, Jackson sat and began the process of slowing his breathing and emptying his mind. Today was a momentous day, and one that he would re-member for the rest of his life. Little did he know, as he sat on the wooden floor of his quarters, that he wouldn't be remembering the date for quite the reasons that he thought.

■ ■ ■

Jackson blinked, but that was his only movement. His job was never done, it seemed, but he remained alert as he looked through the scope of one of his favorite weapons. In his hands was the standard-issue, NAU Marine Corp. M40 sniper rifle. A reliable and versatile weapon that always got the job done. Rising up through the ranks of the Marines, Jackson had come to see his M40 as an extension of himself and rarely used another weapon. He was used to being an elite sniper at this point, but even so, the meeting at Azteca Stadium still had him cautious enough that he was on high alert.

Sweat slowly rolled down the side of his face and dripped onto the concrete floor of the stadium beside him. It was hot and hu-mid, and while his black gear didn't exactly help to cool him down, it was a part of the job. He'd long ago gotten over the discomfort of weather conditions as they came with the territory. The nine years he'd spent with the Marines had felt like a lifetime, and one that was scattered with snow, deluged by rainstorms and burnt out by heat waves.

He was in a crouching position, constantly ready to fire, his rifle partially braced by the concrete slabs surrounding the sta-dium, the weapon ready to find his target and eliminate it almost as soon as he'd seen it. His deep-set oval brown eyes concentrated on his surroundings, searching for anything that just wasn't right, anything that moved or made the hair on the back of his neck stand up. In his ear, there was a small speaker, allowing him to hear what was being said in the meeting taking place on a stage erected in the middle of the stadium. After the explosions of the terrorist's bombs only such places were used for important diplomatic meetings. The government planner liked places where wide areas of open space could surround the politicians, areas that could be carefully watched and threats could be eliminated before they got close to their targets. A lapel microphone along with his ear speaker allowed him to communicate with the other man who was protecting the presidents with him.

Jackson listened to the meeting with mild disinterest on his face that belied his true feelings. The truth was that he was nervous, nervous about the outcome of such a huge decision. The article on the news website that he'd read that morning was the first official confirmation that he'd seen of what was being discussed and what happened below him on that stage would affect him and the lives of most of the world. On the stage was the president of the NAU and the president of Mexico, deciding the fates of millions. Across the stadium was Armani Vasquez, his trainee and, Jackson thought, his friend. They had become close over the last couple of days, training intensively for this moment. Around the stage was a shimmering sea of reporters and cameramen, but those didn't worry Jackson. He knew that each and every person close to that stage had been fully scanned and x-rayed; he had nothing to worry about down there.

Jackson's sharp eyes were honed in on the large area across the arena from himself while Vasquez was watching the side below Jackson. Although Jackson was not looking directly at the stage, he caught glimpses as he scanned the attendees. President Meyers, the leader of the NAU, wore a tailored blue suit that screamed expensive. His red tie was worn as a distinct power color over his crisp white shirt. His simple silver cufflinks gleamed beneath the harsh sunlight. It all fit his persona of power. Even his black hair graying at the temples helped distinguish him. It was dyed that way strategically, as an illusion; few knew that the president's hair was nearly all gray. It was a way to show that the NAU was young but wise. It was one of the oldest tricks in the book, in Jackson's opinion, but it was effective. The president was a traditionally attractive man, in good physical shape despite his fifty-six years. His steely light blue eyes were convincing when political rhetoric came out of his mouth. Few people opposed him, especially in person, because at the height of six foot four, not many could look him in the eye.

President Espinoza of Mexico was a stark contrast to the gleaming North American poster boy. He stood at about five ten and was in his late sixties. His low-hanging jowls reminded Jackson of a bulldog. He also wore a blue suit, but he paired it with a striped blue tie. It was clear that he was tired and making an effort to look much more alert than he actually was. His hooded brown eyes gave him away, and so did the deep, long sighs he took every few minutes. His hair was thinning from above, and was sure to be completely gone in the middle within the next few years. He had been elected only because he was such a hugely different figure from the last president that Mexico had elected. His predecessor had been young, attractive, and corrupt. Mexico wanted a change, and not just in politics, apparently.

Jackson kept his ears attuned to the conversation that commenced. The two men were still exchanging pleasantries; it slightly annoyed him, although he knew it was necessary. He hated being in the huge stadium inside a small suburb of Mexico City. It wasn't because he disliked the location. Actually, he'd become quite accustomed to the country in the few months he'd been stationed there. He'd travelled the entire world during his time in the military, but he wanted to be done. The politics and the constant moving around was taking a toll on him.

The location was a huge nuisance, but President Espinoza wanted to meet on his turf. He wanted to ensure that his military was there to protect him. Ordinarily, anyone meeting with the NAU president would be taken to the White House, and of course President Meyers had wanted the meeting to be in Washington to showcase his own power to the world. However, he agreed to Espinoza's demands because he wanted to show that he was flexible and willing to work with him in the future. Also, President Meyers was the one that wanted something. It was still a quid pro quo world and nothing was free. If he had to do something as simple as go to Mexico for the meeting, then so be it. Still, Jackson thought, he'd have far preferred to be in Washington, watching the cherry trees, safe from this oppressive heat.

Jackson continued to watch and listen, willing his muscles into submission, keeping his mind as quiet as possible.

The pride that he felt from having one of his trainees working across the field helped to ease his stress a little. Knowing that Vasquez was there, knowing his skill as intimately as he did, was a weight off his mind. He knew that Armani Vasquez was as close as he'd ever seen to being the perfect shot, even without Jackson's training. But now that he was trained, Jackson thought, Vasquez might be almost as good as he was himself. Almost.

Vasquez was sharp, and he reminded Jackson a lot of himself. Armani was in his mid-twenties, but he had a hell of a future ahead of him. Jackson remembered the first day of training, the slight hesitation in Vasquez's voice that had betrayed a small lack of confidence. That was gone now. Now Vasquez knew what he could do and Jackson was pleased. The other men had been a job and he'd done it—trained them. Some he liked, some he didn't;

some liked him, others didn't. Most would make decent snipers, if not expert ones. Vasquez was a special case though, or at least he was now—a true genius with his rifle.

Knowing that Vasquez was around gave Jackson the confidence to let his focus slip a little, just a touch, but enough. He thought of his daughters, MacKenzie and Maya, near and dear to his heart as always, though he carried no pictures of them. He never had because he couldn't stand the thought of being captured and someone else seeing his precious girls. His chest tightened as he thought of his wife, or soon to be ex-wife, Courtney. That had been the news in the letter he'd received the night before, the one balled up in the trash can. She was divorcing him. She was sick of his shit, she had written. He was never there so she might as well be a single mother.

Like it was his damn fault that he kept getting sent away. He didn't choose where he went; it wasn't a decision he could influence, and he'd thought that she'd understood that and that she'd wait for him. But they'd only been sixteen when they met and he hadn't dreamed of joining the military then. He'd dreamed of other things, mostly her, and apparently so had Courtney. By the time he'd joined up, they were already married and Maya was on the way. They had agreed it seemed the smart thing to do.

He tried to get Courtney out of his head, but he wanted her back. He wanted to go home and stop her from leaving him. She was everything to him. She and his daughters were the three things that kept him going every day. If he lost her, he didn't know what he would do, or who he would be.

"Jesus, when are they going to get on with it?" Vasquez came crackling through the earpiece, interrupting Jackson's thoughts and bringing him back into focus.

Jackson fought a smirk. It was true, all of the posturing on the stage in front of the cameras was becoming mundane, but it was a necessary part of the diplomatic dance going on down there.

"Stay focused," he said roughly to Vasquez, aware of the irony of his words, meaning the reprimand as much for himself as his student.

"As always," Vasquez sighed.

Jackson inwardly shook his head and bit back a grin. That was another reason that he liked Vasquez: he was never afraid to speak his mind. If he didn't agree with or understand something, he made it very apparent, which helped prevent misunderstandings. It was a valuable skill in a comrade. But he also knew how to follow orders. He may question an order the first time, but he always followed it. Vasquez wasn't some mindless drone and that's what made him one of the best. He knew how to think himself through situations and he did it fairly quickly. That's what it took to be an expert when wielding a rifle. A shooter has to make split second decisions and those decisions don't just mean life and death. The decisions that they made could make peace and war; one wrong decision could cause a catastrophe.

A change in the tone of the voices speaking in his earpiece told him that the meat of the meeting was finally beginning.

"Although I'm happy to have you here, I have to admit that we're on two completely different ends of the spectrum on this issue," President Espinoza was saying. "Our country as a whole doesn't have much interest in joining the NAU."

Interesting start, thought Jackson.

"And that's why I'm here," President Meyers said confidently. "I'm here with the intent of changing your mind. You have everything to gain and nothing to lose in this merger."

"Except for my country," Espinoza said, skeptically.

"Of course, massive changes will have to be made," Meyers soothed. "But this will strengthen us as a whole. We're much stronger together than we'll ever be apart."

Jackson found himself biting his tongue, his jaw stiff, and he consciously had to relax himself. As he listened through his earpiece, sweat dripped from his brow. And it wasn't just the heat of the sun anymore: history was being made on that field below him, and he was present for it, suddenly certain that Meyers was about to get his wish.

Twenty-five years ago, before the Hariq Jihad attack that brought down both the Sears and the CN Tower as well as two ball stadiums, the thought of melding two countries into one empire had never occurred to most people. And yet an empire had been the consequence, and one, Jackson had to admit, that worked well. The NAU, composed of the original fifty states of the United States and ten further Canadian states, was stable and economically sound. The creation of the union had done much to satisfy critics on both sides, with the general population feeling safer and better guarded. Sure, it had been an adjustment for everyone involved and there were some that despised losing their own country, the Apocalytes for one, but both the United States and Canada were relatively new countries in the grand scheme of things so the adjustment had been made.

Mexico, on the other hand, was no new country. It was a land that had once been an empire in its own right, one with thousands of years of history behind it. And yet Meyers was well on his way to wooing the Mexican government into joining the NAU. With a further thirty-one states to add to the union, the NAU would be the largest superpower in the world.

Through the magnifying scope of his rifle, Jackson could see President Espinoza's lips turn up slightly at the corners. "So you want to create a United Continental States of America?" he asked, more rhetorically. "You've been pursuing this issue for quite some time, but if I'm to be frank, I'm put off by the amount of power that the president of such a union would have. It doesn't seem that any good could come from one man being so powerful. And you have forgotten one important thing, President Meyers."

"Which is?" asked Meyers, his face impassive.

"That unlike twenty-five years ago, when Canada was being persuaded to give up sovereignty, there has never been a terrorist attack on our soil. We do not fear the Hariq Jihad as you do, and have no reason to."

Meyers gave a nod of acknowledgment. "That is very true," he said. "However, we have captured many Hariq loyalists in our country, and all of them have come through Mexico. This is the very reason that we wish to join forces with you and shut down the borders to make the entire continent self-contained. We can all win from this. Think about the economic possibilities for a start. And more to the point, just how long do you think that you can straddle the fence on this issue?"

Espinoza's face darkened a little. "That's not a threat, is it?"

"Not at all," Meyers said, quickly and coolly. "I'm merely saying that neutral parties usually have to pick a side in the end, that's all. And would it not be far better to join forces with a country that is close in proximity and that you already have a good working relationship with? Or at least..." He allowed a brief pause here for dramatic effect. "At least I would like to think that we have an excellent relationship."

"This is true," agreed Espinoza. "We have a good relationship. Certain things could be better, as I'm sure you agree."

"Some of those issues will become irrelevant if we join forces," Meyers said.

And now Jackson found himself impressed with the seemingly small Mexican president. Could it be that Meyers wouldn't get his way after all? Meyers was cool, calm and collected, but he'd have expected nothing else from the man who was in the fifth year of his first presidential term. A constitutional amendment had been passed years ago now that extended each presidential term to six rather than four years and allowed a maximum of three terms. The argument had been that in the delicate world of international politics, it was difficult to accomplish anything of note in only four years, particularly when dealing with countries who did not have elected leaders. Diplomatic relations were hurt when these leaders had to start over and over again with new peers.

Espinoza wasn't looking too impressed however, and Jackson thought that he might have underestimated the man. Though, in truth, the president probably just resented the prospect of downgrading his own position. Should Mexico join the NAU, Espinoza, as current president, would, of course, be brought on board as a cabinet member. The NAU cabinet was composed of five members at the moment: the former Canadian president, two former governors of Canada and two former governors of the United States. Espinoza would be an important man, certainly, but he would no longer be the only important man—his word would not be law. Not many powerful people are willing to take a back seat—not after they had clawed their way to the top, after all.

For the next half an hour the two men on stage spoke together, and Jackson found himself ignoring their droning voices as they discussed the same issues in circles. As the conversation moved towards wrapping the meeting up, two assistants, one for each president, ascended the stairs to the stage and stood to one side. Jackson flickered back into focus, keeping his eyes sharp as people began to move. Danger usually struck during chaos, not during order, so if anything was going to happen here, now was prime time. The presidents got to their feet, adjusting their suits as they rose. They stood before one another, preparing to shake hands for the hundreds of news cameras below them. No agreement had been struck. Espinoza had held his ground and voiced his distaste for such an arrangement repeatedly until Meyers conceded.

Then a voice in Jackson's ear piece whispered, "Half left."

It could only be Vasquez, and Jackson quickly began scanning the area as he asked loudly, "What was that?" He was anxious to know what Vasquez had seen, what danger he had identified that Jackson himself had missed.

"Sorry, Jackson...just following orders," Vasquez said.

Jackson had just a millisecond to understand that there was true apology in those words, a sense of regret, or...something un-identifiable. "What do you..." he began, but before he could finish, a shot was fired.

On the stage, everything played out like a film that had been slowed down until it was barely understandable. Meyers fell dra-matically to his knees, and Espinoza crumpled, his body splayed on the edge of the stage.

Jackson acted completely on instinct, and without a hesitation or a second thought, pulled the trigger, hitting the trajectory per-fectly. Vasquez dropped heavily from his vantage point, falling to the grass of Aztec Field.

In the stadium, people were fleeing from any exit they could, pandemonium ruling as screams and cries ripped through the air. All pretense of security was gone; the only thought was for each to save himself. On the stage, things were different; years of long training kicked in as secret service men surrounded Meyers, hud-dling around him to protect their leader with their own bodies. Jackson watched all this through his scope, and when the agents pulled away after the stadium emptied, he saw the president holding his right arm, a smear of blood on his shirt, a graze and nothing more—lucky.

Vasquez didn't share the same fortune, not with Jackson pulling the trigger. As guards hoisted Vasquez's limp body from the ground, Jackson could see the bloodstain blossoming from his forehead. A clean shot, one to make his commander proud, yet why did he feel sick?

And then, strangely alone on one side of the stage, was the body of President Espinoza.

4

THE AFTERMATH

February 18th, 2076

Mexico City

Over the next few minutes, the events unfolding below were in slow motion and then, imperceptibly, they sped up until Jackson felt he couldn't keep up. The haunting picture of the body of Vasquez clouded his vision, and the sad loneliness of Espinoza made him feel physically sick. He maintained his post, turning his scope to Meyers who had blood splashed on his cheek. However, he was sitting calmly on the ground, mostly surrounded by guards. The president was, Jackson understood, waiting for what would happen next, without fear, but with a look of mild curiosity on his face. He realized this was stoicism, and for a second, Jackson thought about what a Marine Meyers would have made.

He needed to examine his own feelings. He knew, from long experience, that this was an essential part of the debriefing required after a kill—one that kept a shooter psychologically sound. He hated it but it was necessary. He took a second to try and gauge his own mental state—proud. He was proud of his president for remaining so brave in the face of near assassination. There was one feeling. What else? Horror. He was horrified at the death of Espinoza. There was another. Surprise. Espinoza's body had a clear head shot, and he was surprised that Vasquez had made such a clean shot by accident. Jackson didn't think he could have done such a perfect job from that distance if he'd been trying to hit the man. It must have been as accident, which meant he shouldn't have shot Vasquez. Jackson felt himself shutting down to avoid processing these thoughts.

He took a long breath and then a second, trying to get a grip on himself. Guards rushed around, medical personnel finally taking to the stage, Meyers standing, still alone, Espinoza lying, now the center of attention. Things weren't as bad as they could have been, and were more relaxed than he would have expected. It took him a moment to figure out why. The danger was gone—there was only one shooter, and he had been disabled; there was no need for top-end security. The shooter was gone because he himself had taken him down. He needed to keep his breathing slow to tone down his adrenaline.

"Holy shit," he said out loud, though there was no one there to hear him. "I just shot Vasquez. I shot my friend. I shot a baby's father."

His friend. Had he really considered Vasquez to be his friend before now? Killing him had been a mistake; he was sure of it. His training was so beaten into him that he had acted on instinct, pulling the trigger when he should have waited to get an explanation. Okay, be logical, he reminded himself, breathing faster. Vasquez shot Espinoza and he didn't know why; only that it must have been a mistake, an accident. He could have attempted to disable Vasquez rather than kill him. It would have been possible. And now his hands were shaking. He kept waiting for something to happen, but nothing was.

Something lurked at the back of his mind, like a dog pacing back and forth. Then the pieces began to fit together. Vasquez killing Espinoza made no sense, which left only two possibilities, both of which involved Vasquez firing on someone else. Either Vasquez had shot at someone he thought was threatening Espinoza and had hit the president by mistake, meaning that there was potentially someone else dangerous still out there, a possible threat that had escaped because Vasquez made a mistake. But as he desperately searched his mind, Jackson couldn't think of anyone else that had been close to Espinoza and could have been a target, except for one person. That left the second possibility: Vasquez hadn't been firing at Espinoza at all, he'd been firing at the other man—President Meyers.

His ear piece crackled to life.

"Get on down here, Jackson," said Grimaldi's voice.

It was time to leave this place—to leave the spot that he'd so carefully chosen earlier that day because it strategically gave coverage over most of the arena. He walked away from where he'd shot his friend—a man who had maybe tried to assassinate his president. Was he still his friend? The question confused him so much that he refused to think about it.

What was going to happen now? He wanted to go home; he wanted out of here and to be with his family, or what was left of it, at least, with Courtney wanting a divorce and the kids. Again, something that he couldn't think about. There were so many things, so many emotions, and if he had to deal with them right now, his damn head was going to explode and then nothing would get done.

His training kicked in. He had needed to kill Vasquez. It had been a necessity. Think about it, he told himself. Just think. He'd taught Vasquez all he knew, including how to get out of tight spots. The man would have made it out of the stadium, he was sure. Looking at the area that Vasquez had occupied, Jackson could spot three different ways of escaping the scene without being caught. No, killing Vasquez had been the only choice, though it hurt his heart. Even injured, the man could have made it far away.

Stay calm. Do what you need to do. His internal voice was calming him, reminding him of his duty, and he was glad to let the emotions slide for a moment, however healthy it might be to confront them. He began to do all that was necessary to leave his spot. He pulled the scope of his weapon and began to take the rifle apart, grabbing his black tactical carry bag. Focus on the task at hand, he told himself. Do what you need to do.

He was a sniper, the handles on his carry bag worn down from years of wear through all kinds of danger. Somewhere between forty and fifty different targets now, so one more shouldn't make a difference, shouldn't make him hurt the way he did. With so many kills under his belt, he should know, did know, that it was kill or be killed. He knew exactly how many people he had killed as a Marine, and knew that he had to keep going just as he had after any other mission, had to do what was necessary or things were going to end badly for him. God knows he didn't want to end up screaming and ripping his hair out in some damn veteran's mental hospital. But it happened, even to some of the best. It wouldn't happen to him though. He was going to deal with this like with any other death—just one more to add to the count. What was one more baby-faced, young, smart, funny man—one more father?

Vasquez would make the forty-seventh kill he'd made in the field. And he was going to be the last. As he zipped up the carry bag, Jackson vowed to himself that Vasquez was going to be the last. He just couldn't do it anymore; another one might break him. He had to go out there and find a new place to be, a new thing to do, a new talent to use. He just wasn't being helpful anymore. After killing Vasquez, whether the man was his friend or an assassin, he felt like a murderer, not a hero. It was just the way it would have to be. He wanted out—to leave the forces—and now he had a concrete reason not to go back.

There was more, he thought as he shouldered his bag and got ready for the climb down. Maybe this would be enough to make Courtney happy. Maybe she'd accept this as his sacrifice and let him back into her life. After so many years and so many deployments, he was ready to let this career go. He'd do what he had to do in order to get an honorable discharge, but there was no way he could keep doing this.

■ ■ ■

Cameras flashed, blinding him as he stood on the small stage, a podium in front of him. His face was emotionless, his uniform hastily retrieved from his quarters, but clean. He didn't want to be there, but when the President requested your presence, you didn't say no. At least Jackson didn't say no.

The press conference was a necessity, apparently, necessary to show something Jackson couldn't understand. Maybe this was a way to show everyone that the president was alive. Turning a little, Jackson assured himself that Meyers was very much alive, his arm in a sling now, but dressed in yet another of his immaculate suits, smiling for the cameras. At least, Jackson thought, he hadn't been required to say anything. Just having his picture taken as the hero of the hour was enough. He had a new shiny medal that had just been pinned to the front of his uniform.

More flashes went off, and Jackson felt his face aching from keeping its blank expression. It had been only a couple of hours since he'd left his spot above the stadium, but he'd had time to piece things together, to think things through. Espinoza had been dead on arrival at Mexico City's largest and most prestigious hospital, as had Vasquez. Already Vasquez's face was plastered over the internet and television screens, touted as a traitor, as a secret underground Hariq Jihad operative. Any positive things the man had done were already tainted, though he was only two hours dead.

Why hadn't he seen it? Flashes and shouted questions that he didn't have to answer rang in the background while he kept cycling the day through his head. Meyers spoke for the both of them, commending his heroism. He was just doing his job—doing what he'd always done—killing people. Hardly heroic, was it? Why hadn't he seen that Vasquez was up to no good? He racked his brain, but try as he might, he couldn't come up with a single warning sign. The two had spent a fair amount of time together—were friends—as close as two men can get in a short amount of time. He'd become friends with the enemy, and that was a tough pill to swallow. What was worse was that he mourned him, and couldn't help himself. He found himself missing the man that he'd had to kill. Seeing Vasquez's face everywhere made him remember this, and then...something felt wrong about it. Something felt wrong about Vasquez being equated with Hariq Jihad, but he wasn't sure what.

The applause of the crowd and a further rush of camera flashes snapped him from his thoughts, and he suddenly found that the president was offering him his hand. Painting a cordial smile on his face, he took Meyer's hand and shook it, eliciting another flood of camera flashes.

Christ, he wanted to go home. He wanted his family. He wanted the hell out of here. And all the while he clasped hands with Meyers, praying and wishing for this all to be over.

■ ■ ■

Days had passed from the day of the shooting. President Meyers and his delegates remained in Mexico awaiting a transitional government change. Jackson therefore, remained on security detail, with plenty of time to think. He'd come to terms with what he'd done, somewhat, though it still made him uncomfortable to think about it. He was simply too well trained to regret his actions permanently. Vasquez as traitor still didn't sit well with him, though he couldn't quite put his finger on why. It was just so unlike the man, he supposed. The one thing that bothered him was that he'd deliberately passed over Vasquez as a commander of the mission team because he'd judged the man to be a follower rather than a leader. Yet he'd been independent minded enough to be an assassin for Hariq Jihad? It could have been a judgment mistake, Jackson thought, and he didn't like making mistakes, but everyone made them sometimes. He had never made a mistake before in judging the character of a man under his command though, so it irked him that he'd finally fallen prey to ill judgment in his last tour of duty.

He left yet another debriefing meeting and paused in the courtyard, enjoying the warmth of the sun after the cold air conditioning. He was very ready to leave Mexico—ready to go home. He appreciated that Meyers was taking advantage of a desperate situation in order to get what he wanted. A transition government would be weaker than a real one, meaning that Meyers was more likely to get the agreement that he wished for. Sticking around was the right thing to do, or at least the smart thing to do politically.

Menendez had been vice president under Espinoza, and was now acting president, likely to become transition president any time now as the country waited for his position to be ratified so that they could proceed with a new election. Only a president could announce an election, meaning that there were hoops to jump through before things could get moving. Menendez was a lot less decisive than Espinoza had been, needing more time to make decisions, never quite sure of what he should do. Jackson had seen him in action and noticed that while the man made certain to ask questions of his advisers and to poll opinions, he ended up going with whatever was the popular thought at the time. If Meyers was as smart as Jackson knew he was, then he was simply waiting for Menendez to be ratified so that he could pressure him into an agreement with the NAU. With Mexico still reeling from the assassination of her president, the safety and security of joining the NAU was a big selling point. Smart, thought Jackson.

His thoughts were interrupted by a private, coughing beside him. Looking up, Jackson saw an unfamiliar young man trying to capture his attention.

"Yes, I'm Sergeant Jackson," he said, cutting off the man before he could speak, used to being a famous face by now. "And yes, it was me you saw on the TV with President Meyers."

The private blushed, a red wave flooded his cheeks and his eyes darted to the side as if searching for a way to escape. Jackson suddenly realized that he'd misread the situation and couldn't help but laugh.

"And...that's not why you want to talk to me, is it?" he said, chuckling and putting the private at ease.

"Um, no sir, sorry sir," said the man, nervously. "I am sup-posed to escort you to President Meyers's quarters, sir."

"Really?" said Jackson, raising a questioning eyebrow. "And I don't suppose you know why, do you?"

"No sir," said the private.

"We'd better go and find out then," said Jackson. "Lead on!"

He allowed himself to be led into the building, a large colonial style mansion that had been taken over by the president and his staff, not to mention his security forces, for the duration of their stay. It was a nice place, thought Jackson, the terracotta and earth tones making the rooms seem cool and spacious. The ceilings were at least fifteen feet above the floor, and fans slowly rotated above. The overly effective air conditioning pumped out frigid air. The warmth of the sun was forgotten and he shivered a little as he kept step with the private.

"In here, sir," said the man, finally, stopping in front of double doors. "The president is expecting you."

"Thank you," said Jackson.

"And, if I may say so," said the private, "you were great on TV."

Jackson was still laughing at the man's cheek as the private left, and then wondered what he was supposed to do. The president was expecting him, so did that mean that he needed to knock, or just walk straight in? He decided to take no chances and knocked once before opening the door.

"Ah, Sergeant Jackson," said Meyers as the door opened.

He was sitting behind a large desk piled with papers and didn't get up, instead gesturing to a seat on the opposite side of the table.

"At ease, Jackson," he said. "With all you've done for me, you will never have to salute me again. Grab a seat, I've been meaning to talk to you, and I've finally gotten a free moment to do so."

"Sir, yes sir," said Jackson, still a little wary of how he should behave.

The military had taught him that he was supposed to be standing at attention, and yet here was the president of the NAU telling him to sit. He took the chair, but sat upright, not letting his spine rest on the back, as a sort of compromise between formality and friendliness.

"First, I wanted to inform you that I will be giving you the Presidential Medal of Honor when we return to Washington, in return for your service," began Meyers.

Jackson narrowed his eyes a little, confused. "But you have already given me a medal," he said, without really thinking. "Another really isn't necessary; I was simply doing my job."

Meyers waved a hand at this. "Nothing really to do with that. I know you were doing what was necessary. But a nice, shiny Presidential Medal of Honor Ceremony will make me look good as well as you, and more importantly, will be one of those occasions that people cling to—to help them heal after a disaster and all that. You know how these publicists work."

"Sir, yes sir," said Jackson, bowing his head, though he really had no idea how publicists worked, but he could see the president's point.

"Second, I also wanted to ask you to become a part of my security detail full time," continued Meyers.

Ah…'ask' was probably the wrong verb in this circumstance, thought Jackson, knowing full well that he wasn't being asked, but was being demanded. This made him cautious. "I'm not sure how well that will go over with my wife," he said, tentatively.

Meyers frowned. "Aren't you and your wife progressing towards a divorce?" he asked.

"Well..." Jackson stammered, pausing to gain his composure. "Um, well, yes, but how do you know, sir? I mean, I haven't told anyone."

"I'm the president," said Meyers, looking serious. "I know everything. I have access to information that you would never believe. Knowing your marital status was hardly a challenge."

Jackson swallowed, and then was startled to see Meyers's mouth twitch until the president was laughing.

"I kid," Meyers said. "I was told that you've been on active duty for years now. I assumed that there would be some kind of marital strain—there nearly always is."

Jackson let go of a breath that he hadn't realized he was holding. "I honestly thought you were serious there for a moment, sir."

Meyers laughed harder. "No, no," he said, finally. "But I was serious about the position. Will you take it?"

Feeling a little more at ease, Jackson took a moment to think, before replying: "In honesty sir, I'm not sure. I was about to leave government service."

"Well, your government still needs you," said Meyers, sternly. Then, relaxing a little, he continued: "Besides, you have to do something if you're not wandering around teaching people how to shoot, and it might as well be something that you're good at, like security. You won't need to travel; I have an away team for that, so you'll be based in Washington and will stay close to the cabinet. You'll have damn close to a normal life. Might be enough to cheer up that wife of yours."

"I'd have to move," Jackson said, thoughtfully. "We're based in Chicago right now."

"New city, new start," said Meyers. "Trust me, your wife will jump at the prospect of moving towns, settling down, and getting to live in DC. So, what do you say? We have a deal here?"

"If I can get my wife to agree, then yes, I suppose that I'd accept, sir," said Jackson.

He desperately hoped that the president was right about Courtney, and that she'd agree to move and maybe even stay with him. He couldn't face the prospect of having to go to Washington and leave his precious daughters with their mother in Chicago.

"Good," said Meyers, standing up and offering his hand. "I'll even do you one better, soldier. When we get back to the states, I will personally talk to your wife on your behalf. I think it will be hard for her to say no to me."

Jackson stood, too, noticing that Meyers had an unnervingly rough grip, not like the typical, firm government hand shake. His hands were rough and strong, like he spent his days doing manual labor. He wanted to ask why, but knew he couldn't—knew that the question would sound odd.

"Now, if you wouldn't mind, I'd sort of like the man who saved my life to follow me around. At least until we get back to the Union," Meyers said, releasing his grip.

"I can do that, sir," affirmed Jackson.

"Then let's go," said Meyers, rounding his desk. "I've got to get Mexico to join us."

5

THE AGREEMENT

This time, to Jackson's relief, Meyers had insisted on a closed room. From a security point of view, this gave Jackson a more confined space in which to protect the man. While he understood the theory of a large space making it easier to isolate, he preferred defending an enclosed room. There were fewer people involved as well, with just a handful of assistants. The room was airy and relatively open, and the windows were made of safety glass so Jackson didn't worry too much about them. The requisite safety scans had been done and there was no sign of bugging equipment or explosives. The room itself was comfortable with a large conference table as well as several sofas and easy chairs. The art work on the walls was mostly abstract. Courtney would like the painting over the mantel particularly, Jackson thought, with its bold colors and thick lines. He wondered how much it would cost but decided he probably couldn't afford it on his salary. On his new salary though...who knew?

While initially he'd assumed that the smaller venue was for increased security purposes, it soon became clear to Jackson that security wasn't exactly on Meyers's mind. In fact, as the new Mexican Interim President walked into the room, Jackson suddenly had the feeling that Meyers didn't want anyone to hear or see what was about to happen. A look flashed across the president's face, one of...what was that? Arrogance maybe, and Jackson felt slightly disturbed.

Menendez had been ratified as interim president just hours ago, and was still bouncing with pride. He was a tall and elegant looking man, dressed in a designer suit, his shoes shining and hair perfectly combed. Jackson thought he could detect a hint of make up around the man's eyes, but he wasn't sure. Whether he used cosmetics or not, the man was obviously proud of his appearance, a bit of a peacock even.

Meyers on the other hand looked powerful as usual, even a little intimidating. Jackson watched as Meyers greeted Menendez, gripping his hand until Menendez winced at the pressure. He guessed that Menendez wasn't used to that farmer's handshake either.

"Let's not beat around the bush," Meyers was saying. "Take a seat, Menendez, let's talk."

Menendez looked around and an assistant hastily reeled something off in Spanish, until a look of comprehension dawned across his face.

"Ah yes," he said. "I was not familiar with this 'beat around the bush,' but I agree. We shall talk."

The two men took seats on opposite sides of the large conference table, and began to discuss the future of their two countries, avoiding the pleasantries and small talk that Jackson had noted at the first presidential meeting. Jackson himself stood alongside the wall in a corner a little removed from the action, although he could hear every word being said at the table. His eyes scanned the room, assessing the threat levels, careful examining each of the men that had entered the room with Menendez. For whatever reason, Meyers had decided to take only Jackson into the room with him, but Menendez had two assistants, plus a security detail at the door. Meyers had two men outside the door himself, and Jackson guessed that all of this was a show of power on Meyers's part. A way of advertising that the NAU wasn't afraid, and that nothing would stand in its way.

Not for the first time, Jackson wondered at the possibility of Mexico joining the NAU. From a diplomatic standpoint, he understood perfectly, and whether he liked the idea or not agreed that it made sense. However, as he watched Meyers speak, he began to understand that this was personal. It was about more than diplomacy, it was about politics and, even more, it was about Meyers himself. Why, he wondered, was Meyers so damn set on getting Mexico?

The more he considered the question, the more complete the puzzle became inside his head. Currently, the Union was doing fine on its own. The economy was strong, people were relatively happy, security was acceptable, and the NAU was a powerful player in global politics. But, he thought, Meyers needed more than stability, didn't he? What Meyers needed was votes. If he wanted to remain president of one of the most respected superpowers, then he was going to need people to vote for him. Stability and continuity alone didn't impress people. People didn't like to hear about results being the same as the previous quarter, they wanted improvements. So if Meyers wanted votes, wanted to remain president, then he needed to improve things. Adding Mexico into the mix would be a pretty big improvement.

As he watched Meyers, he could almost taste how much the man wanted this. He was allowing Menendez to speak, was cool and collected and apparently listening. Yet Jackson saw how much this man embodied being the president—how he reveled in his own power and authority. For a moment, Jackson understood how intoxicating it must be to hold that power.

Menendez was still chattering away, his English far from perfect but acceptable, and Meyers was watching, listening, nodding occasionally in a polite fashion. Jackson wasn't following every word of it but it was something to the effect that Mexico had worked hard to remain separate from the US since the Mexican-American war of the 1800's where significant territory was lost to America. General Juan Morales, who fought to save Veracruz, was an ancestor of Menendez's, so he was not about to give up what his family had battled for so long ago. Menendez eventually finished, his point made, and looked satisfied with himself. When Meyers began to speak, his voice was so low that Jackson had to strain to hear it but his tone was unmistakable.

"Here is what is going to happen," said Meyers, quietly but firmly. "You are going to join with the North American Union in order to form the United Continental States of America. You will be made vice president of the Mexican District in return."

It was obvious to Jackson that this was no offer; it wasn't a deal. Meyers was simply telling Menendez how things were going to be. This was no longer a negotiation—it never really was. Meyers's voice was steely, and his eyes looked hard. Jackson found himself a little afraid of the man and his drive.

"I'm not...so sure about this," stammered Menendez in his hesitant English.

Meyers still looked calm, his words were even and measured. "You have no choice," he said. "There is no way that Mexico will survive without the support of the NAU."

"What do you mean?" Menendez asked, innocently.

"I mean that, as soon as I close our borders with you due to the increased risk of Hariq Jihadists coming into the NAU through Mexico and place a trade embargo on business with Mexico due to the clear indications that your cartels are funded by Hariq Jihad, then you'll be without a lasting trade partner. Your economy will be unable to survive the blow."

Meyers said all this as though explaining a homework problem to a five year old. There was no threat in his voice, no meanness, and yet that was unnecessary. The threat was in his words, and Jackson shuddered internally at the thought of the power his president wielded.

"I do not think that you have the authority to do such a thing," stuttered Menendez.

The man opposite him smiled, a wide, shark-like smile, and put his hand to his breast pocket, withdrawing something. "I have here a pen," Meyers said, idly. "I can make an executive order cutting you off in the name of protecting the homeland."

"You...you cannot do that!"

Meyers raised his eyebrows and shrugged. "I can and I will. To protect my country, I'll do anything that I have to do."

"I just...I just don't know."

It was clear that Menendez was beginning to lose it. All this was too much pressure for a man who wanted nothing more than to be the center of attention, admired and groomed. He was losing his nerve and looked around as though seeking the comfort of his assistants.

"Oh, you do know," said Meyers. "You just don't want to admit that you already know what you're going to do. And let's face it, a member of the Hariq Jihad just shot your president. Without the help of the NAU, the terrorists will tear your country apart, and without our trade, your citizens will tear their own country apart. In the face of all that, the only place that your people will turn to is the organized crime in the cartels as they can provide black market goods. Increased support for the cartels will mean the end of your government anyway, so you lose nothing by joining with us."

Menendez swallowed, his tanned skin looking sallow, sweat beading on his brow despite the freezing air conditioning. Jackson was so anxious that he could barely stand still, witnessing the most amazing act of manipulation that he'd ever seen, stunned at the power of Meyers.

The silence stretched for several seconds before Meyers allowed his face to soften a little. With a hint of sympathy in his voice, he said, "As presidents we are forced to make difficult decisions every day. It all comes down to one thing: we must do what is best for our country. No matter how hard a decision seems, it's easy if you keep that in mind. Simply choose what is best for your nation, and according to that criterion you have no choice but to join us."

Menendez looked at Meyers and then dropped his eyes to the ground. Jackson could tell that the battle was already won though not a word had been uttered for several minutes by the Mexican president. Meyers sat back in his own chair, relaxed and comfortable, waiting for Menendez to find his tongue. Menendez turned his chair away from Meyers, breathing harshly while speaking quietly with his assistant. Jackson leaned in a little, wanting to hear what the man was whispering, but it was in Spanish and he didn't understand more than a few words.

With a sigh, Menendez turned his chair and lifted his head. "I will be the president who killed our country," he said, to no one in particular. Then he turned, almost looking Meyers in the eye but not directly because he was no longer the alpha. "Okay."

"Okay?" asked Meyers, pressing for full vocal affirmation that he'd done what he'd always dreamed of doing.

"Yes," said Menendez, more formally. "We shall join with the North American Union."

Meyers nodded, and turned briskly back into the businessman that Jackson had always seen before. "Excellent," he said. "We have the necessary treaties and documents prepared, of course. I'll see that your people get them in the next hour or so. We'll get everything signed in a press conference tomorrow and let the world see what we're all made of, yes?" He gave a quick laugh here to punctuate his words. "And then, well, then we'll meld us all together. The United Continental States of America—it has quite a ring to it. We will be a nation unrivalled in all the world."

Menendez looked pale and shaken, and Jackson recognized all the signs of shell shock. He shook his head slightly, despairing at what had happened. No one should be forced into such a decision—it should be done for the right reasons rather than to placate a bully.

Meyers stood and flashed Jackson a wink, looking ecstatic as he did so. Meyers wasn't the kind of guy who took no for an answer, Jackson thought, and for a moment, he had a queasy feeling about agreeing to work for the man. If he could force a president to give away his entire country, what could he do to a simple soldier with a wife and family at home?

■ ■ ■

The documents forming the single nation of the United Continental States of America, or the UCSA, were signed the following morning in front of news cameras from across the globe. President Meyers looked happy but business-like, while President Menendez kept his head down as he added his signature to the papers. When he was done, he suddenly looked up as if realizing that, as of that moment, he was no longer president. Sadly and slowly, he placed the ceremonial pen back into its holder before turning to shake hands with Meyers.

Jackson was standing in the background, observing as always, eyes peeled for potential threats, in clear view of all the cameras. He was hoping that somewhere his wife and children were watching—that they could see him on television and be a part of this, too. He hoped that seeing him here with the president, making history, would be enough for Courtney to fall back in love with him and be proud of him for all he had accomplished.

There were a barrage of photos taken, lights flashing; Jackson stood silent through it all. How strange it was, he thought, to see history being made. This was such an important moment and yet he didn't really feel any different. As remarkable and amazing as it was to watch the UCSA signed into being, he could still think only about his family.

President Meyers was moving towards a central podium now, preparing to give the speech that he'd spent much of the previous few weeks working on. Jackson tuned most of his full attention to his leader while continuing to monitor for threats, and listened intently to his words.

"People of Mexico and the North American Union, or as I should now call you, new citizens of the United Continental States of America, I come to you today to speak of a new nation—a nation that has been conceived in honesty and integrity, and one that will embody those ideals forevermore. This will be a nation that will make us all stronger in the face of those that oppose us, one that will protect us all in the fight against the increasing threat of the Hariq Jihad and any other group that would dare stand against us."

He paused and looked around the room, letting his words sink in while another round of pictures were taken, cameras snapping as he smiled. Then he cleared his throat and went on.

"No longer must we be afraid of the terrorists who seek to sneak into our country, crossing the borders in the south, and filing one by one into our land. No longer will we be held hostage to our anxieties. We will halt these people now by closing and policing our own borders along with our brave allies of the old Mexican state, and we shall create a stronger country. A country where we shall all sleep safe in our beds at night. A country that is greater than any other, greater than any that has ever been. It will be one in which we may all live at peace—a country that we can call the United Continental States of America. United. As one together."

Again, that photogenic pause, and Jackson marveled at how Meyers could hold the audience in his hand, controlling the way they reacted to him. It was truly a wonder. Then Meyers nodded, and the speech went on. A speech that one day would appear in history books.

"I speak from my heart and from personal experience. As you well know, just days ago, a terrorist had a direct impact on my own life. A man who I will not even give the respect of naming attempted to kill me and, in the process, extinguished the life of President Espinoza. I was lucky, but a great man was not. And make no mistake about it, President Espinoza was a great man. He cared for his country and wanted what was right, just and best for the people of Mexico. I am sure that, given time, he and I would have come to a very similar agreement to the one signed here today. Fortunately, President Espinoza was followed by another great man, a man that you see before you today, Interim President Menendez. It was his wisdom, strength and courage that allowed this treaty to proceed, his insistence on carrying out the real wishes of President Espinoza, out of respect, and making our two great countries into one."

Far from looking like a great man, Menendez was looking like a broken one, his face pallid, brow sweaty, and eyes circled in black. Jackson felt a stab of pity for him, a man obviously unqualified to hold the position that he'd had—a man forced into greatness and then bullied into signing away that greatness. Meyers's voice was rising to a crescendo now, reaching the apex of his speech.

"As one country, we can do so much, and we will live our lives without fear. We will never wonder if the enemy is coming to us from the south or the north, we will strengthen our borders and keep our great country safe. We will police those borders in ways never seen before; we will keep ourselves protected from the likes of foreign terrorists that want to claim and desecrate our soil, and make it impossible for them to enter our country, and they will turn away, beaten."

There was a roar of approval at this from the audience, but Meyers still wasn't done. His eyes were flashing now, and Jackson had observed him long enough to know that whatever else had been said, whatever had been promised or done, it was what was about to come that was most important. Whatever was to be said next was going to be the real meat of the matter, and he found himself leaning forward in anticipation despite his distaste for the situation.

"We will protect ourselves from the likes of the Hariq Jihadists, and from all enemies, both domestic and foreign, and we shall do so in the most secure ways possible. In the next few months, I will roll out changes that are designed to protect us all—changes that will keep our children safe in their back yards, our mothers safe in their beds. The way things are done in the UCSA will change, sometimes dramatically, but in only the best ways. The first of these great changes will be a Second Alien and Sedition Act, which will shore up our borders in order to keep us all safe from the Hariq Jihad. This will also be designed to protect us from enemies within our own country, protecting us from those with seditious intent."

Although he mentioned no names, Jackson knew that he was talking about groups such as the Apocalytes, those that vocally disapproved of the way the government ran the country. He wondered how effective this new Alien and Sedition Act would be. Only time would tell, he supposed.

"With this act," Meyers said, his voice rising yet again, coming to the grand finale and still controlling his audience with finesse, "We will become one mighty block. We will always protect ourselves. We will isolate ourselves, but isolate ourselves together. We shall be as one. We shall live in peace and without fear. We shall care for each other and love each other, and our great country shall survive. We will not just survive, but thrive! And our enemies shall perish! Starting tomorrow, I will start the process of bringing back all of our troops from abroad. We will no longer be the enforcer for other countries' wars. Our fighting men will not risk their lives for another country. For centuries, our great military acted as a police force for other nations. If they couldn't do what needed to be done, we would step in and do it for them, and other nations would hate us for it. Even our own citizens protested against it. No more. Our men will be here to protect us and us alone from all enemies both foreign and domestic."

Meyers gave a quick pause to let it sink in. "That leaves only one thing to say," Meyers said, his voice quieter now. "God bless the United Continental States of America!"

The crowd erupted, everyone coming to their feet and cheering, some crying from the great emotion of it all. Even Jackson found himself clapping. It had been a brilliant speech, and who didn't want to be free from the clutches of terrorist bastards like the Hariq Jihad? This would keep everyone safe—it would keep his family safe. Maya, MacKenzie and Courtney could sleep better at night. Even his new job would be easier. For a brief moment, Jackson believed that everything was going to be better. He'd get his wife back, his children would worship him as a hero, and his country would thrive as promised. All because of the genius of one man. President Meyers was the best thing to ever happen to this country.

His hands stung from clapping, his ears ringing with cheers. At the back of his mind, a little voice reminded him that Armani Vasquez was one of those terrorist bastards and that Menendez had been threatened into signing away Mexico's sovereignty. It said that Meyers was a whole lot more terrifying than he appeared. But Jackson quickly silenced the voice and went back to applauding even louder than before.

■ ■ ■

In the days that followed President Meyers's speech, things moved faster than expected. Meyers rapidly signed a number of executive orders, having taken a hastily written oath that allowed him to act as president of the UCSA rather than only as the president of the NAU. One of these orders was the promised Alien and Sedition Act II, which was more or less as it had been outlined by Meyers himself. Another was the Protection Act, which made it effectively illegal to enter the UCSA without the explicit permission of the new head of ICE, which was the renamed Travel and Immigration ministry. In general, Jackson applauded these moves, thinking it was exactly what the country needed. He was starting to enjoy reading his morning news and anxiously opened the news app during breakfast. Controlling who came in and out of the country seemed like the only sensible way to protect the citizens of the UCSA, at least in the short term, and surely these were to be temporary measures. The one thing that Jackson hoped would be permanent was keeping the troops within their own borders.

The effects of these mandates were frightening, though. Troops abroad were accosted by civilians in war-ravaged countries, begging them to stay. Where there had been relative peace, insurgents were taking over in anticipation of the UCSA troop removal. In some cases, the troops fought back, but most were already on their way home or respecting their orders to detach from any situation not directly threatening their own lives.

Numerous ships were sunk as illegal immigrants attempted to get into the country by water and were fired upon by the UCSA navy. Jackson supposed this was to be expected, as the lines must be tested; he suspected that after several weeks the incursions would stop. Immigrants had to learn that the only way into the UCSA was the legal way, and that they would risk death by trying anything else.

On top of that, citizens now needed permission to leave the country, something that caused a certain amount of grumbling. As soon as Meyers signed the Protection Act, all foreign travel was stopped, including travel by UCSA citizens themselves. Airlines with international flights complained so loudly that the government compensated them financially for losses, as they had to not only refund thousands of tickets but also lost new revenue on future flights.

It was now necessary to put in a request to the Bureau of Travel and Immigration in order to get permission to leave the country. Currently, the wait time was about six months to get approval to enter or leave the country. However, Jackson thought that this was probably only because it was a new process, and that faster, more effective procedures would soon be set up.

It did seem that the government was growing increasingly suspicious of people who wished to leave the country though, which could be seen as a little unreasonable. Questions were asked: where are you going? What are your plans? Why don't you want to vacation within the UCSA? It would, after all, be easier for everyone concerned if citizens would just vacation inside the UCSA, at least until the situation was stabilized.

Regardless, it was important, Jackson believed, that the people understood the needs and position of the government. The people of the UCSA needed to stand together, and the government's main priority at the moment was protecting her citizens. If that meant pissing a few people off because they didn't get their European vacation this year, then so be it. All the government was trying to do was keep things safe and protect the people from the horror of what lurked outside their borders. Jackson was well aware of what was awaiting people in other countries; he'd seen examples of it himself. Countries that had not followed the model of the UCSA by fighting and outlawing terrorist movements had experienced immense changes, pain and suffering.

France, for example, had been under siege from the Hariq Jihad for years and was now a divided nation. In what had become almost a repeat of the Crusades of a thousand years ago, religious war raged across the country. The French government had only recently pleaded with President Meyers for aid from the UCSA to help them defeat the terrorists that were slowly taking over their country. About half of the land was now under the control of the Hariq Jihad, and in cities, people lived in constant fear. Militant Jihadists progressed rapidly through the rural areas. People tried to live their lives like normal, to do their jobs, but it was near impossible when terror controlled them.

Much of France was ruled by Sharia law where the Jihadists reigned. The French governmental security forces had either been forced out or taken over by the Jihadists. Many police units had disbanded or retreated to larger cities, trying to hold parts of France together. Journalists likened it to the ancient fiefdoms of the Middle Ages. A religious leader was appointed to control the town—to observe and enact the law, punishing as they saw fit. Jackson shuddered at the thought of anything like that happening in the UCSA—of his daughters being subject to such barbaric laws. It must be hell for those living in France, and for their neighbors too—those worried that the Hariq Jihad plague could spread to their own land.

People hoped for the best rather than taking action, as the UCSA had done. The French had pleaded for help from the UCSA, but in the end, President Meyers had refused. He did not want to involve the UCSA in yet another foreign quagmire, had more than enough of his own security issues to deal with, and was unwilling to risk voter popularity by sending valuable UCSA soldiers onto foreign soil. Jackson could hardly blame him for what seemed like a very sensible decision.

France wasn't the only country having problems. All over the globe, people were suffering, whether due directly to terrorist groups or not. The United Kingdom, whose economy had generally weathered quite well in the past, was now experiencing a harsh recession. Critics blamed the UCSA for this due to the loss of foreign trade from the closing of UCSA borders that had also severely affected economic markets elsewhere. Others suggested that the recession was due to the problems in France, traditionally a valuable market for UK goods, and still others said it was simply the way of the economy, an inevitable economic cycle. Everyone had a theory, although no one was sure of a cause or solution.

The benefit of this was that the people of the United Kingdom were desperate to leave their country, and where else would they want to go other than the United Continental States of America? As much as they tried, they were consistently denied entry visas for the UCSA. The policies that Meyers and Congress set forth kept foreigners out to avoid a subset of the population that may burden society. The migrant issues in Europe of 2015 were a lesson that the UCSA took to heart; Meyers wouldn't get reelected if foreigners were living in UCSA stadiums and camps. Despite long historical ties with many countries including the UK, Brits and other Europeans alike were not allowed to enter. As the economic situation in the UK worsened, there were protests and calls for the UCSA to provide amnesty and support as the rest of the world faced starvation, poverty, and war.

Yes, Jackson felt bad for these people. He also knew that it was a moot point, and there was little to be gained in grieving about something that he could not change. There was nothing he could do about the situation, and even if he could, he wasn't sure that he would. As far as he was concerned, desperate times called for desperate measures, and Meyers was making solid decisions right now. On a daily basis, he heard Meyers say that the country had to protect itself, and he was a believer. He had a family to protect; what else was he supposed to believe?

6

THE FIRST YEAR

June 20ᵗʰ, 2076
Chicago, UCSA
Article Originally Published in the *Chicago Herald Tribune*, Reused with Permission
    Graduation Ceremony Displays Impressive Patriotism
    Jessica Hemphries, Local News Correspondent
On Friday, June 19ᵗʰ, 2076, Baxter Memorial High School's class of 2076 graduated to thunderous applause. The class, consisting of just over 400 students, is the first group of Chicago high school students to graduate in the newly-formed United Continental States of America, making an already special day more meaningful.

Made official on Thursday, May 18ᵗʰ at midnight, the North American Union officially became the United Continental States of America (UCSA) as Mexico declared itself a member of the union. Mexico, who recently suffered the tragedy of a presidential assassination with the shooting of President Espinoza just days ago, quickly decided to become the second sovereign country to join with what was once the United States of America as soon as the ratification of Interim President Menendez allowed them to legally do so. May 18th will become a federal holiday, in accordance with the tradition set for September 5th, the official federal holiday marking the date on which Canada joined with the United States to form the North American Union.

President Meyers, who was instrumental in bringing Mexico into the Union, was among those praised during the Baxter High graduation ceremony. The graduating students of Dwight Baxter Memorial High School displayed exemplary amounts of enthusiasm in giving a rousing and patriotic ceremony. The graduation ceremony began with the recitation of the new Union Salute, a brief spark of humor in an otherwise stirring and emotional night, as understandably many were unfamiliar with the new salute.

The Salute, written by Poet Laureate Winston Bismark, reads as follows:

> *In solidarity with my peers*
> *I pledge allegiance to*
> *the unity of our many states*
> *A country of many*
> *joined together to*
> *become one.*
> *The United Continental States of America*
> *shall forever stand.*
> *United by diversity and*
> *strengthened by similarity*

Next, salutatorian Mikki Kendo sang the national anthem of the North American Union, commenting that this would be the last time the auditorium would hear the hymn, followed by a very well-sung rendition of the recently prepared national anthem of the United Continental States of America.

This was the first time that most of those present had heard the new national anthem, and many were moved to tears. The most memorable lyrics were certainly: "from sea to sea, from day to night, for our great country we shall all fight." The words drove home the message that "our new union will not lie down in the face of terrorism," according to one audience member.

This was an allusion to the recent fatal shooting of Hariq Jihad operative Armani Vasquez of Mexico by Sergeant Anthony Jackson, a previous resident of Chicago. Jackson, who was recently honorably discharged from the NAU Forces, has recently accepted a posting to work directly with President Meyers on the president's security detail, likely in recognition of the hero's fatal shot that killed the assassin of President Espinoza and saved the life of President Meyers. The move is seen as not only a solid appointment for national security but also as good public relations. In fact, the names Anthony and Jackson have both gained rapid popularity in the last weeks since Jackson was announced as a Presidential Medal of Honor awardee.

The family of Armani Vasquez could not be reached for any official comment, though JMC news, in an ambush of the beleaguered family, captured a cryptic comment from Mr. Vasquez, Armani's father, "It was not supposed to be him." This statement was given in response to one of the many questions that the family were being bombarded with. However, due to the sheer number of questions and Mr. Vasquez's refusal to respond further, it is unclear to which question this comment was in answer.

Conspiracy theorists have suggested that Mr. Vasquez was speaking in response to the question: why was your son trying to assassinate President Meyers? While other conspiracy theorists have suggested that the father was not responding to any question at all but was instead suggesting that the son was not supposed to have died.

It is important to note, however, that none of these conspiracy theories appear to have any grounding in reality. No evidence has been provided, and many of these theories are known to have come from groups that are opposed to the government such as the famous Apocalytes.

Baxter High's graduation ceremony had a number of well regarded speakers, one of which was a surprise to all. Former Interim President of Mexico, Alvaro Menendez, gave a rousing speech after flying in by helicopter, one of his first official duties as co-vice president. He spoke to students about the importance of vigilance as they continued out into the world, particularly in the face of the increasing violence of terrorist agencies.

June 20th, 2076
Somewhere over the Continental UCSA

Jackson barely glanced at the article, catching only Menendez's name and wishing he could have ridden to Chicago with him. Instead, he had been transported to Texas through military channels to catch a commercial flight home. He barely even noticed the references to himself, embarrassed to see his name in articles lately.

Returning home was a monumental moment in Jackson's life. A month of sitting in Mexico, waiting for the President to stabilize the situation and go back to DC, had been difficult for him. He could now become the person he had long dreamed of being—the doting father, maybe even the loving husband if he played his cards right. He was so excited that he could barely contain himself, and he'd jumped on the first available flight out of Mexico

City as soon as the President had given him permission to leave. He couldn't help but hope. He knew that things weren't going well with Courtney, knew that she wanted to divorce him, but he also knew that it was all because of the distance. Things would be better when he got back to Chicago. She'd see that he still loved her and everything would go back to normal, and then he could tell her about the move to DC. God, he hoped she was as excited about it as he was.

He stretched out his legs as far as he could in the cramped airplane seat. He hadn't wanted to wait for any kind of special treatment, even for a business class seat to open up. He just wanted to get home. Patting his breast pocket, he felt the papers tucked safe inside—the official discharge papers. He'd picked them up as he left as evidence to show Courtney. This time, she would know that he was absolutely and completely done with the forces and home for good. It wouldn't be like the last few times when he'd been home just long enough to see his daughter born, for a long weekend, or for Christmas, and then he'd just disappear back off into the distance. This time would be different.

Once, long ago, Jackson had thought about being a career man, but the idea had paled in comparison to being a family man. He needed to prove to Courtney that was what he was. He knew that she hated him risking his life, hated him being gone all the time, especially now that they had kids. But to be fair, he thought, he had done it for her. At the time, joining the military had been the only way they could support themselves and a new baby.

He didn't think that Courtney underestimated him, though— didn't see him as a dumb soldier like many people did. She knew that he was a man of fierce loyalty, dedicated to the NAU, or the UCSA, as he was supposed to call it now. Everything he did was either for her, or their family or country. He had just saved the president's life. You didn't get much more loyal than that. He hoped he'd made her proud.

Vasquez. It still weighed on his mind. He'd met the man's parents once, when he was still the commander of Vasquez's training unit. They'd seemed nice, and he felt sorry for them. He'd like the chance to apologize to Señor and Señora Vasquez, he thought. It seemed like the right thing to do. He knew they wouldn't forgive him; he wouldn't forgive the person that shot his child, but it needed to be done. He would do it in person, not in a letter or a call. He vowed to himself that he would go back at the next opportunity and apologize in person to Vasquez's parents as well as to his widow and daughter.

Widow. How glad he was that Courtney had never had to hold that title. A stewardess came with an offer of drinks, but he didn't take her up on it. He let his mind drift, silencing all the other voices, letting the plane fade into the background as he thought about her. Her long brown hair and deep green eyes. He remembered the way she always smelled like freshly washed blankets and how she joked that that was a terrible thing because it just meant she'd been doing too much laundry. Her smile was perfect, with straight, even teeth—big and deep, full of vibrant life. Her smile lit up any room and made him so happy he could hardly stand it. He smiled to himself now, just thinking about her.

He was struck by a terrible sadness, like a knife through his heart, as he remembered her letter, asking him for a divorce. She said that she couldn't handle being married to him anymore. He knew that he needed to take care of things, fix the issues that had made them drift apart. With his discharge papers in his pocket, he felt that he'd taken care of her main argument for leaving him. He would never again put the military ahead of his family. He was tired of that life—always being on the go, never knowing where you would rest your head the next night. It was a life that many men and their families learned to adjust to, and he would have gladly welcomed Courtney supporting his lifestyle, but she just didn't have it in her. He couldn't blame her for that.

Originally, she'd been anxious about moving around so much, wanting to give their children a steady place to live and to go to school. There were thousands of conversations spanning the length of their marriage where she fantasized about living in the house that she'd brought her daughters to after she left the hospital with them for the first time. Life didn't work that way as a military wife.

They'd rented their first real house together when they'd found out that Courtney was pregnant the first time, and then they'd spent hours going through ads until they found the perfect house that they wanted to buy. It had been expensive so he'd signed up with the Marines in order to make the down payment. Back then, he'd had no big career plans, and the Marines seemed like fun. They went through two more houses in rapid succession as his base changed. Then he started sniper training, and all thoughts of getting out of the forces were gone. He'd finally found the thing that he was good at, even great at, and he loved it—being talented, respected, and given the opportunity to think for himself. He'd loved it so much that he immediately agreed to another tour of duty once his training was finished, and Courtney had gotten very angry at him for the first time. She'd yelled, screamed, and cried that she didn't want to move so much. She'd sobbed that she didn't want him to be away all the time. But in the end, he'd convinced her, persuaded her that it was an honor to serve their country, that he would be careful. Where else could he use that training in civilian life and, besides, he would quit after this next tour.

He hadn't quit though. He became one of the best snipers that the forces had, and when he'd come home from a tour and placed his hand on Courtney's belly, swollen big as a balloon with their second child, MacKenzie, he'd felt a thrill of excitement at the baby but dreaded what was about to come.

Sure enough: "Don't do this again," Courtney had said. "You said one more tour; now it's done, so quit please."

He'd shaken his head. He wasn't done yet, wasn't finished doing this. "I've got to continue," he'd said. "It's best for all of us. We need the money now, and we'll need that military pension later. With number two here on the way, it really is the smart decision."

It was important to him to be able to provide for his family, coming from an impoverished background. He didn't want to give his children the same upbringing.

"We don't need the money," Courtney said, her eyes welling with tears. "What if you don't come back?"

"No. I'm not going to have my family live in poverty as I did. We're going to have money," he'd told her, obstinately.

"We need you, not money," she'd begged.

"And what kind of father would I be if I didn't bring home money?" he asked her, knowing that he was being proud and stubborn.

"I can work, too!"

"Court, you should be able to stay home with the kids—look after them, be a mother. I don't want you to have to go out to work."

"I want to work."

Now she was being stubborn, and he was sick of it and close to losing his temper. He knew that he was doing the right thing, that providing for them all was the right thing. So he stood up, ready to storm out of the house.

"We're not having this conversation," he said, angrily. "I've already re-upped with the Marines anyway, and there's no getting out of it. You're just going to have to learn how to deal with all this."

"But..." she trailed off, dissolving into heart-wrenching sobs.

He felt bad so he went back to her and put his arm around her, stroking her hair and holding her. "No buts," he said. "I'm going to be fine."

Now, on this plane, thinking about a life without her, Jackson wished that he'd listened to her. Things could have turned out very differently. He could have stayed home with Courtney, been there for MacKenzie's birth. At the time, he was so certain that he was doing the right thing, doing what he needed to do for the sake of their daughters. As much as Courtney protested, they did need the money. He figured later he would be there for them. He'd work, get his pension, and then they'd have money and they could have him too.

However, it had killed him to be away from them all, though Courtney didn't always realize that. He hadn't even known about the birth of his second daughter until days later because he'd been out on a mission. He desperately regretted not delaying his re-enlistment. It would have been magical for him to have been there for the birth of his daughter. Now, whenever MacKenzie asked him what it was like when she was born he couldn't tell her, had to tell her to ask her mom or her grandmother because he hadn't been there.

He could tell her about how he'd been out in the desert, trying to protect his unit from insurgents and suicide bombers of the Hiraq Jihad, but she wasn't much interested in that. Yet he knew that he had done a good thing as well. He was protecting his country, and therefore his family, while paying the bills at the same time. This might have been the right thing for him, and even for his girls, but it might not have been the right thing for the woman that he loved.

He continued like this for a while, leaning back in his plane seat, wondering what had been the right thing to do then and now. There was, unfortunately, nothing he could do to change the decisions that he had already made. If he could go back in time, would he change them? Well, maybe buying a house wouldn't be so important to him; they could have lived in an apartment for a while longer, he guessed. He could have worked a couple of jobs at a time, rather than re-enlisting. Maybe they could have gone up to the Northern provinces and roughed it for a while.

There were plenty of oil jobs up north. The Northern provinces, or what was formerly known as Canada, were full to the brim of oil and oil products. Oil had been the top national export since the pipeline had been built. Back then, he hadn't realized how lucrative oil jobs could be. Mind you, an oil job would also have meant being away from home a fair amount so maybe even that wouldn't have satisfied Courtney. He hadn't known much about his choices at all, if he was honest.

He was sure of one thing though: if he'd have known then what he knew now, he'd damn well have been in that room to meet MacKenzie when she made her first appearance.

Going back in time could be useful, he mused. Would he go back and refuse to shoot Vasquez? Now there was a tough one. One for another plane ride maybe; he was getting sick of analyzing everything. Besides, his plane was beginning to bank. Looking from the window, he could see Chicago spreading out beneath him. He could see the spot light in the sky, shining from the memoriam where Wrigley Field once stood—a constant reminder to the entire Midwest of what the Hiraq Jihad had done to their great nation.

As the plane touched down and taxied towards the gate of O'Hare (semi) International Airport, Jackson was both thankful and happy to be home. All he needed to do was grab a cab and get to his home in Naperville. In an hour or so, he'd be at home with his wife and children. His heart raced at the idea. Then a thought struck him. He hoped she'd be at home. He hoped Courtney would let him stay there. He hadn't really locked down any living arrangements...

He walked from baggage claim with his duffle in hand. He looked over at a man holding a sign that said, 'Gunnery Sergeant Jackson.' He was astounded that someone had sent a limo for him. He approached the man hesitantly, "I'm Sergeant Jackson."

When he approached the car, he noticed it had the seal of the President of the NAU on the side. President Meyers had sent it for him. In the back of his mind, he thought that was the least he could do.

The ride home wasn't very long, but his heart raced the whole time. How would Courtney approach him? What would he say? When they pulled up, his stomach dropped and he was as nervous as the day he had asked her to marry him. He took a deep breath and opened the door. Before he could exit, Maya and McKenzie ran into the car screaming "Daddy!" and jumped onto his lap. Courtney was in the background holding her hands over her mouth and crying. He tried to stand from the car but the girls wouldn't let him up. With all his strength, he stood up and held each girl in an arm. He smiled at his beautiful wife as tears flowed down his face. She ran to them and embraced them in one big hug. "I'm so glad you're home. Forget that letter, forget everything in the past. You're my hero and I love you. President Meyers is inside waiting for you and he told me everything. I think us moving to Washington is a great idea."

June 30th, 2076
George Washington Elementary School, Chicago, UCSA

It was the last day of the school year, and Jackson entered the foyer of George Washington Elementary School to see his daughter Maya graduate from sixth grade. It was a meaningless ceremony, Jackson thought to himself, but he couldn't say anything out loud, since it was the first time in a long time that he was with his family. Courtney wasn't yelling at him and everyone seemed at least moderately happy. The entrance to the school confused him and for a moment he wondered why, then realized what was odd. Why, he wondered, would a suburban elementary school need x-ray machines? He saw the same machines at every airport he'd ever been to. He read once that they were installed after the first terrorist attack on American soil back in 2001. What could they possibly be worried about inside a child's lunch box?

It seemed stupid to him that they would be worried about such things as terrorists in a school. He believed with all security measures put in place within the UCSA that the children were very safe and secure. He focused on the graduation rather than his righteous indignation.

He made his way to the school gymnasium, decorated nicely for the ceremony, and found Courtney sitting up in the bleachers, saving him a place. He walked up to her and sat down, looking around at all the other seated parents, and then down at the middle of the gym, where around fifty boys and girls sat dressed in their Sunday best. He grinned over at Courtney, MacKenzie's little blond head in between them, and was rewarded with a smile in return. He hoped that was a sign of things to come.

They all three searched the crowd for Maya, looking for her distinctive dirty blonde hair, and the pretty blue ribbons that Courtney had tied in her pigtails. She was wearing a dress of sweet robin egg blue, and they found her sitting in the fourth row. Jackson guessed this was because they sat in alphabetical order, but maybe that was just military thinking. He flicked through a program that had been left on his seat, something that was reminiscent of a high school or even college graduation. Jeez, they were really going all out here for the sixth grade. Taking themselves a little seriously, he thought, but then, maybe the kids appreciated it.

He didn't want to detract from something that was important to his daughter, and knew that his attitude was everything. His family had kept a close eye on him since he'd returned, waiting for the inevitable signs that he wanted to leave again. Courtney took him back, though he was currently sleeping in the guest room until they were reacquainted. He was cautiously hopeful that things would be back to normal soon. Mind you, she'd said the same thing when he'd asked her before his last deployment if they could try for another baby. As soon as the deployment was scheduled, she had said no.

'Think about it' could be a code word for 'no,' so he wasn't fooling himself. This was still going to be an uphill battle. He did have a few things going for him. He'd saved the president's life, for one, and there was something about being a life-saver—not to mention the life-saver of the president of the most powerful country in the free world—that melted away distrust and anger. He hadn't heard a single word of complaint about who he was as a person since he'd arrived home.

Her pleasantness may only have been because he had finally given in to her, though. There had to be something about a man who was willing to give up his profession, the thing that he was good at, just for her happiness. Did that not have some weight?

He was willing to change his life for the love of his life, for Courtney. It wasn't like it had been when they'd first got married. He had enough skills now that he should be able to walk into any security-based job that he wanted. Besides, he had a firm job with the president, one that he thought she would approve of. Nevertheless, he didn't really know what was going to happen. He decided playing the role of the doting father and husband would be best for now.

He tried to refocus his thoughts, holding MacKenzie's little hand in his own, as the ceremony began. The first thing that happened, as was traditional, was that everyone stood to say the Pledge of Allegiance. Jackson was a little perplexed as to what was going on as a large banner unfurled from the ceiling with a large portrait of President Meyers on it. It seemed a little weird to him, but everyone else took it in stride, so maybe this was perfectly normal. Besides, he didn't want to make waves, not today, so he kept his mouth closed.

Everyone began to speak in unison, and then Jackson discovered yet another problem. He had a little trouble saying the new Pledge.

"I pledge allegiance to the fla..." he began, before realizing that this was not what anyone else was saying at all.

He stopped speaking and just moved his mouth, letting the gathered crowd continue the pledge without him. It began nearly the same, he was satisfied to note, as he listened to people chanting:

"I pledge allegiance to the United Continental States of America and to its leader, who protects us from enemies, both foreign and domestic. I pledge my loyalty to the country and vow to help the government in the fight against our enemies."

The pledge struck him as strange, but he didn't want to be a boat rocker. Besides, it was new and unfamiliar, and maybe he would get used to it with time. Jackson thought that he'd have to remember to learn the new pledge so that he wouldn't feel like a complete moron the next time he was at a school function. He wondered how long these pledges had been going on: he couldn't remember many times that he'd had to pledge allegiance once he'd graduated from school. Maybe there was a handful of times in the military, but not many. So it probably wasn't really that important anyway.

He let his eyes rove over the audience. People sat and paid attention, and maybe it was just him, but he felt that everyone was on eggshells. He remembered once going to a graduation ceremony of a friend and spending most of the time gossiping and chatting with others, not paying too much attention to what was going on until the big moment arrived and his friend got his diploma. But then, these were little kids, maybe parents just wanted to set a good example. Maybe.

He smiled a little to himself. He was surrounded by his family and that made him happy. It made it easier to forget about all that had happened before: easy to forget Vasquez's face, strange pledges, and everything else. Pretty soon, he knew, everything would be back to normal. He just had to figure out what he needed to say to Courtney to get her to let him in her heart again. Sure, she agreed to go to DC for a fresh start, but still, she was distant.

From the corner of his eye, he watched her. Just what was so great about her? Aside from her looks, it was tough to pick any one thing that he loved about her more than another. He loved the way her hair flowed down her back, an elegant ribbon decorating the style. He loved how playful she could be, teasing and child-like. Yet she could also be sensitive, serious, nagging even. He liked her contradictory nature and that was what had attracted him to her in the end. It was certainly what kept them married because she continued to surprise him every day. There was no chance of him ever becoming bored with her. They had been estranged for too long. Today they would go out for ice cream, he decided. It had been a family tradition in his own family, and he was going to make it one for his daughters.

He knew that things weren't ever going to be the way they had been in the past, and that all that had happened between him and Courtney couldn't just be wiped away and forgotten. He wondered if he could persuade her to go and get ice cream with him, or even if she'd allow him to take the girls. He knew, deep down, that she loved him.

The children were preparing to do a dance for the parents, an intricate dance that Jackson thought he wouldn't be able to do himself. Mind you, dancing had never really been his thing. He should learn. Maybe he and Courtney could take classes together, have a common interest. That sort of thing was supposed to help troubled marriages, wasn't it? The children looked a little nervous, smiling and yet downright terrified. He couldn't see Maya, so instead he focused on a small, blond haired girl who was in the middle of the group, her feet delicate and graceful. She reminded him of how Courtney could have looked as a child, and the thought made him smile again.

The girl wore a red dress, red as a fire truck, and was dead center in the group. With the red dress, blue tights and a white headband she was almost a little flag. At least he thought so—assuming, of course, that the new UCSA flag wasn't all that different from the NAU flag that he knew and loved. Then the dancing stopped, though the music continued, and the children grouped together and looked to be waiting for something. Someone, somewhere must have given them a sign, because suddenly they began to sing.

> *Praises to our president*
> *He who is heaven sent*
> *Hath saved us from destruction*
> *Gave us a resurrection*
> *Stopped the men with bombs*
> *Protects us all a long*
> *Forever while we live*
> *Forever while we live*
> *Praises to our president*

And so it went on, and on, and on. An endless stream of verses continued, and Jackson began to wonder if the song actually had an end. All the verses extolled the virtues of the president. Jackson was annoyed, mostly because he was ready to get the hell out of here and to get ice cream with his family, but he didn't want to leave because it would disappoint Maya and because leaving during such a show of patriotism could be construed as, well, disrespectful. There was another, niggling little worry. All this personal worship, he'd seen things like this before; he remembered the cult of the leader from studying dictatorships in high school.

It all reminded him of North Korea, back when it had still been a country, the way they idolized their leaders, made them the center of their nation, whether that leader was good or bad. He was happy that North Korea no longer existed; the state had eventually collapsed and had been peacefully taken over by the more technologically-advanced South Korea to become Korea. Some had worried that it was all a ploy and, that once reunited, the old North Koreans would use their influence to return the entire nation to its fascist roots, but it had never happened. People had had a taste of freedom and were unlikely to go back to the way things had been before.

They sat and waited, the dreadful song finally coming to an end, and a litany of speeches occurred. Finally, a list of names was read by a tall, thin woman who he suspected was the principal. As they waited for Maya's name to be called, he watched child after child get a paper—not a diploma but something called a certificate of completion. He was, of course, happy that Maya hadn't had to stay back and repeat sixth grade or anything, and happy that she was smart and healthy. But still, was it really necessary to have these ceremonies for sixth graders?

Jackson was used to accomplishments actually meaning something. He'd been a Marine and a top sniper during a time when it hadn't necessarily been important to be one. Wars had been winding down for years and the world wasn't as dangerous as it had once been, at least for NAU citizens, despite the terrorist threat. Nevertheless, he knew that they had needed him in order to keep the country safe. He'd provided a service that not too many other men could provide for their country, and he'd been extremely good at it.

Being a sniper was just one of those things that he knew how to do better than anything else he had tried to do. He was happy that he knew how to do this thing, no matter how mysterious it was to him, how strange it was to have a natural ability and have no idea where it came from. He'd never expected much of a reward for doing his duty as a soldier, other than his pay check and assurances that his family would be taken care of. He wondered why this generation of children should be brought up to believe that they were owed accolades for the small things they had done in the world. Graduating sixth grade was hardly a major accomplishment, after all. By rewarding this, they were simply bringing up a generation that was going to become dependent on small rewards rather than work because they had to. It made him mad. He kept his daughter's image in his mind and heart to ground him. He kept thinking about how proud she felt and how happy this ceremony was making her. This wasn't about his feelings, it was about hers, and he needed to remember that. If not for her though, and for the sake of his ailing marriage, he'd have walked right out of the gymnasium.

So, he watched and waited for his baby girl to graduate from sixth grade. Soon she'd be moving on to middle school, and then high school, and eventually college and a career. She'd live the dreams that he had never had the chance of attaining, and she'd have a happy life—all because of the sacrifices he had made for her and her sister. He just wished that Courtney could see things the way that he did.

■ ■ ■

He stood at the door of the house with Courtney. They'd spent the whole day together getting ice cream as he'd planned and catching a movie. It had been almost like old times. He'd enjoyed himself and they'd all laughed, and he'd even thought for a moment that everything was fine. But now, standing at the door, it was obvious from the look on Courtney's face that she was expecting him to back track and head over to the guest room over the garage rather than coming in to the main house.

He needed to know what he could do to fix all the time that he'd missed out on, all the time that he'd given to the military and his country instead of to his family. He remembered his father telling him, "You're gonna lose that girl if you don't put her first." That had been his dad's advice on his wedding day, and he'd thought that the old man was just busting his balls, but as it turned out he wasn't. The old guy really knew what he was talking about, and since he'd had twenty years of marital experience Jackson wondered why he hadn't believed him in the first place.

All he wanted right now, just in this moment, was to be with his family in the house they had bought together. The two of them had been a family, even before the kids, and then as the girls came one by one, they had expanded their love and his heart had grown. He wanted to be a dad again. He wanted to be a husband again. He needed it, needed it like air; he was suffocating without them but couldn't see a way to fix it, not right now.

"I guess I should get on over to the garage then," he said.

MacKenzie was pulling on Courtney's arm, wanting to ask her something, but her face darkened as she heard her father's words. "Mom, I want dad to come hang out for a while," she whined.

Courtney frowned at her daughter, but then sighed. "So, you wanna come in?" she asked, being wry about it.

"Sure," he said, trying not to sound too happy but grasping the opportunity anyway.

He stepped through the door. If he could have frozen time just at that moment, his life would have been complete. He hadn't been so happy for a very long time.

He waited to see what would happen next, but nothing much did. He watched a little TV with the kids, but it was close to their bedtime; they were both tired and a little cranky. Courtney handed over bedtime duties to him, and he was ecstatic to read his daughter's bedtime stories and to tuck them in.

Jackson kissed his daughters goodnight, waiting until both had heavy eyes and were almost asleep. He marveled at how beautiful they were and how privileged he was to have them. Aware that he was probably ending his little fantasy evening, he decided he'd better go back downstairs and get ready to get out of the main house.

He popped his head around the corner of the kitchen door and saw Courtney taking sips from a steaming mug that had 'We Love You, Momma' written on it. He could smell the pungent aroma of coffee.

"So, um, drinking coffee?" he asked, uselessly, putting his hands into his pockets and shuffling his feet on the laminate floor. Since when had talking to Courtney become so awkward?, he wondered.

"Yeah," she said, then sighed. "Want some?"

He nodded, and sat down across from her at the table while she fetched him a mug and some coffee. He loved this moment, wanted to bottle it up and drink it, but knew that it would have to end sometime. He had to talk, had to try explain things to her.

"You know," he began, unsure now of what he was going to say and hoping that the words would come to him. "I just wanted to say that I'm so sorry for choosing money and the job over you and the girls so many times."

Courtney stared at him from across the table, her green eyes unreadable, her face a little shocked. She had nothing to say, looked taken aback, as if this wasn't a man that she knew at all.

"I just, I just..." he hesitated and then plunged in to the sentence. "I just got so worried that you guys needed money and needed to live a certain lifestyle, and I can see that I got carried away. I lost sight of what was really important.

"I don't expect anything," Jackson said, cupping his coffee mug in his hands. "I just had some time to really think about the situation when I was over there. I mean, you probably aren't even too thrilled that they offered me a job in Washington working with the president. I know you put on the show for him when he was here. You just wanted to appease him. Maybe this job is too close to the military for your way of thinking. But I just, well, I just thought you deserved to know that I was sorry. I couldn't let us go on like this for much longer with you, well, with you not knowing how truly sorry that I was for putting the job first."

"I don't know," she said, shaking her head slightly. "I just don't know anymore."

"You don't have to know anything," he told her, looking down into the creamy brown coffee. "There's nothing that you need to do. I don't expect anything from you, but I just wanted to say sorry. I can't live with the fact that I put so many things ahead of you all any longer. I was just trying to take care of you the only way that I knew how. My dad was never really there for us, and certainly not when it came to taking care of a family. I wanted to be the exact opposite..."

"Honey," she sighed, wanting to interrupt what could become an argument.

"No, listen," Jackson said, trying to make his tone more reasonable. "He drank everything away. Even when he did work, which wasn't often, he'd spent everything before he got home. But my mama, she didn't care—loved him too much, I guess. So instead she worked her fingers to the bone trying to keep us all clothed and fed, and she couldn't. At least half the time she couldn't, and we went to bed hungry. There were roaches and mice everywhere, and damned if I didn't consider eating them more than once when I was lying in bed with my stomach rumbling, empty and complaining. Knowing that I was giving you the opposite of all that was all I needed to get me to sign up for re-enlistment again and again."

"But why have you nev..." she began.

"Because it sounds so shameful," he said. "You knew we were poor, but you never knew how really poor we were, and I didn't want you to. I was embarrassed of it all, ashamed, and the only thing I wanted was to give you a different life, something more than that."

"I'm...I'm sorry," she stumbled over the words, and he saw that there were tears in her eyes. He hated the pity, but loved her for having such empathy. "I'm sorry, Ant, you should have told me."

"I know," he said, quietly. "I know that now."

"You should have let me know, so that I could have understood why you did all you did—so that I would have understood why you were going out on all those dangerous missions and so determined to be out there busting your ass for all of us."

"I know," he said again. "I should have. Telling you what was going on with me would have been the best route to go; I see that now. But I was just too proud. Even now it was hard to say those things, and I almost wish I'd never told you. I kinda feel like you're sitting there, judging me, thinking about how terrible a person I must be." He could barely look her in the eye.

"Listen, Ant," she said, reaching her hand across the table. "I might have grown up in a family that was a lot better off than yours, but I'm not some kind of heartless monster."

"I know," he said, almost smiling. "I am just so damn embarrassed."

He dared to stretch out his hand too, so that their fingers were just touching, feeling her warmth.

"There's no reason to be embarrassed anymore," she said, pulling his big hand closer so that she could hold it in her own. "I understand. I understand that all you were trying to do was to protect us and keep us safe. I understand that you were just trying to give us a life that you didn't have. Just wish you'd said something sooner. I feel terrible for not giving you the benefit of the doubt, for thinking the worst of you. For not being more understanding, digging deeper, finding out what was going on with you instead of just thinking about myself."

"But you were thinking of the family, too; I get that," he said. "Just we were thinking in different ways is all."

"Oh, Ant," said Courtney.

She got up from her seat and walked around the table, wanting to console him, putting her hands on his face and bringing his head close to her body so that he could feel the warmth of her through her thin cotton shirt, which made him press his face even closer to her, wanting to be a part of her. She pulled him in tighter and he could feel her heart beating and knew her every emotion, how she was feeling and what she wanted.

He lifted up her shirt and kissed her milky white stomach, the skin soft and fragrant. Then he caressed her back and started to stand, his lips making their way up to her mouth.

"Oh, Ant," she said, again, though it was more of a moan this time.

"Court," he said, kissing her soft, pink lips and hoping but not sure, not definite yet. Not until she grabbed his hand and led him down the corridor towards her room, their room. It had been over a year since he had sat on their bed, let alone lain upon it. They kissed as they walked into the room, brief pauses in their journey, until they made it inside and closed the door. Jackson savored every kiss.

They'd have a lot of explaining to do to the kids in the morning, he thought. But as Courtney kissed him again, he figured he'd have enough time to think about that later.

■ ■ ■

It was a couple of days before Jackson had cause to think about politics again. He remembered the Second Alien and Sedition Act, of course, but like many UCSA citizens hadn't been too affected by it. Other than to think that Meyers was doing what he had promised to the best of his ability by keeping the country safe. There was still a constant threat of Hariq Jihad attacks in the country, though there hadn't been many attacks in the UCSA in recent months.

This did seem a little strange when he thought about it. Not that he did for long, but if he had to analyze it, he'd say that the reason no Hariq Jihad attacks had landed in the UCSA, despite Jihadists constantly being caught on UCSA soil according to the papers, was simply down to the great power and leadership abilities of President Meyers. In fact, he even felt a little bit bad about wondering why nothing bad had happened, since that essentially meant that he was expecting negative situations. He didn't spend a long time thinking about the problem though; he was far too concerned with his family, his blossoming relationship with his wife, and his upcoming new job.

Jackson was overjoyed that Courtney had embraced moving with him to Washington. He wanted to be sure that she was interested in their new life, the one that he wanted to build for them. No, the one that they would build together, he reminded himself; the days of him taking sole responsibility were over. Courtney had made it clear that if things were going to work, they would have to communicate far better.

While they would have to move, it wasn't as though that was going to be a hardship. The girls were still young so it would be easy for them to make new friends even though they were being uprooted. Since Maya had just finished sixth grade and would be going to a new school anyway, the timing couldn't have been better. It was an excellent time to make changes in their lives, and it would be the new start that their marriage needed to survive in the way that Jackson wanted. So when Courtney came downstairs one day with an idea, he was anxious to hear her out.

"Ant, I was thinking, maybe we should go ahead and check out some houses in DC right now—have a look around, you know?"

He smiled at her enthusiasm, which was gratifying, but then had a thought. "But the girls still have a couple of weeks of summer camp, don't they? They're having such fun; I don't think they'll be too happy about a trip to DC."

She frowned. "Good point," she said.

"But..." Jackson had an idea of his own. "Why don't you go ahead for a couple of days and have a look around. I can stay here with the kids and give you a break. You could meet up with your cousin, do a little shopping, have some grown-up time."

Courtney's face lit up. "Really?" she said.

"Really," he nodded.

He wanted her totally on board with this idea, and he liked the idea of her having a look around. Plus, he liked the idea of a little down time with the girls by himself. This was the way a family should work, the way his family would work.

The plan was all set, but wary of the new regulations about interstate movement, Jackson figured he'd better make a call and ensure that Courtney got the permission she needed to go to DC.

What he thought would be a small chore actually ended up taking him an entire afternoon, and at the end of that afternoon, he was still no closer to getting Courtney interstate travel permission.

By enforcing the borders between states and requiring travel permits to go between them, the government could accurately track where everyone was, could prevent terrorists moving between states, and keep tabs on everyone. Not a bad idea, and Jackson could definitely see the benefits of it. What he didn't understand though was the vast amount of bureaucracy involved.

Just like with foreign travel, people had to apply to the Department of Travel and Immigration to get permission to go to a different state, whether that was relocation or just simple travel. Jackson knew that with a job offer from the president himself, he was unlikely to have any problems getting permission to go to DC. But apparently Courtney was another matter.

The lady on the phone told him that it would be a minimum of six months before any such travel permission could be given, leaving Jackson fuming and confused. As he talked to more people, he realized that the process of getting travel papers was excessively difficult. Rather than assuming that you had nothing to hide and were being forthcoming with your information, the DTI assumed that all citizens were shadow members of the Hariq Jihad until proven innocent. And while in some cases it had been made easier to travel between neighboring states if you had interstate business, like truckers, in most cases getting approval to cross state lines was very difficult.

He finally slammed his phone down in frustration and was wondering how he was going to tell Courtney that her trip was off. He also wondered how the hell all this was going to function in reality. It would take months for the average family to even plan a trip to see a relative in a different state. That was hardly efficient.

Still, he reminded himself, it was in the name of state security. Just as he was thinking this, his phone rang.

"Anthony Jackson?" said a voice on the line.

"Yes."

"This is President Meyers's office," the voice continued, though Jackson didn't recognize who it was exactly. "We've been informed that you were attempting to get interstate travel permission for you wife, is this correct?"

Jackson hesitated for a moment, wondering if he was in trouble, but then reluctantly agreed that it was correct.

"In that case, please accept our apologies for the delay. For some reason, the names of your family members had failed to pass through the system. Rest assured that your wife now has full interstate permission for her trip. And should either of you require further permissions, they will be granted within twenty-four hours of the request. Sorry for the inconvenience. Please call the White House directly for any future travel needs. President Meyers also instructed us to send a secure vehicle to pick Courtney Jackson up from the airport and be at her disposal throughout her trip. Have a great evening."

With that, the unknown voice hung up, leaving Jackson wondering how the hell he was supposed to feel. On the one hand, he was happy that Courtney was going to DC now. On the other, how did the president's office find out so quickly that he was applying for permission? But being able to get permission immediately was pretty convenient. Maybe it was all to do with security clearance, he decided, since he and his family must have been subject to security checks if he was about to work with the president.

Shrugging off his earlier frustration, Jackson smiled and went off to find his wife to inform her that her shopping/house hunting trip was good to go.

7

THE SECOND YEAR

November 2nd, 2077
Washington DC, UCSA
Article Originally Published in the *Union Standard Weekly Journal*, Reused with Permission
Do We Even Need an Election Day?
Millicent Nieves, Political Correspondent

With Election Day coming up and the postponement of last year's voting, many voters may be concerned that the voting booths will remain firmly closed due to constant threats from Hariq Jihad. However, considering the progress made by President Meyers in this current war on terror, it should come as no surprise to most that re-election of the sitting president will be a mandate. A straw poll taken just yesterday finds the seven out of ten people on the street have not even heard of the president's challenger, Kenny Tsen.

No offense to Mr. Tsen, but his candidacy is a mere formality. It's already clear to all, political pundits and the public alike, that there is no chance of Mr. Tsen winning the presidency, and yet the election process itself needs a challenger in order to appear legitimate. But is it legitimate at all? Is the election process itself a formality? There is an argument to be made that the president should be appointed rather than elected. Even without terrorist threats to close down polling booths, many issues could be resolved by the simple expediency of allowing President Meyers to continue into his second term of office without the formalities of an election at all.

One sound reason to appoint a president based on skill and experience in government rather than by election is to avoid the phenomenon known as Mob Rule. A majority of voters may vote in a candidate who makes promises that please citizens, and yet these promises may not be possible or even legal to keep.

Consider the era of segregation during the mid-twentieth century. The majority wanted separate seating areas for blacks and whites, separate drinking fountains even. Does that mean that the right thing to do was to bow to popular preference, rather than to do what was legal? It took the government to correct this injustice through appointed leaders rather than through the will of the people.

Special interest groups also taint the voting process, essentially undermining the educated voter. Organizations such as the National Rifle Association spend millions on television advertisements, influencing low-information voters with half-truths on gun statistics in order to allow anyone to own a gun, including terrorists. These same groups donate millions to candidates so that, when elected, these candidates can remove responsible regulations regarding gun control to make more money for groups such as the NRA and therefore put ordinary citizens in danger. Appointing a president would ensure that the candidate in question would not be tainted by these special interest groups and would be able to govern without bias.

When a voter casts a vote for their candidate, they are essentially voting for laws based on predetermined morals that they both share. In essence, whenever a voter agrees with any social ideologies a presidential hopeful has, they are voting to control ideas and lifestyles they despise. For a long time, voters restricted the rights of LGBT individuals because they deemed this group immoral. This mindset is not only arrogant, but is also hateful and judgmental. Who are we to judge others who were born with different ideals and biological necessities? That makes us no better than the Apocalytes. An appointed president would understand that we must constantly seek social justice and equality for all citizens of the UCSA. The president must uphold the oath that all Americans are born equal and that we have the right to pursue happiness (something that even Apocalytes will support).

There are responsible Americans who read the internet news every day, watch cable news and who stay up to date with and educated about current events. When Election Day comes around, these Americans are informed through their research about candidates and their ideas. Unfortunately, these responsible ones are in the very small minority and their vote usually gets cancelled out by another voter who is casting his vote simply because it's Election Day and campaigns have told them to head out and vote. In some cases these people are even voting for a candidate's party, without knowing the name of the candidate himself.

Many citizens come out to vote in a presidential election and choose candidates across the ballot from the same party. For those who at least know the candidate's name, they tend to get their information from thirty-second advertisements or flyers through their doors that denigrate opposing parties with misinformation. If the candidate in question happens to be good at fundraising, then they will receive more money, which leads to more advertisements and flyers that can end up guaranteeing a victory. A presidency is bought and paid for.

A good debate performance can also make or break an election. The leader of the free world is chosen based on how well he or she performed on the debate team in college. Any position can be justified if presented in an appealing and misleading way.

Finally, the wealthy pick candidates themselves through political contributions and the rest of the country can have no illusions that they have a choice in the matter. While there are limits to these contributions, the affluent can also donate to non-profit organizations who supposedly have no bias and yet who also spend their money on political advertisements. Earlier this century, an outcry against wealthy donors made some headway with the denouncing of the Koch brothers, George Soros, and Michael Bloomberg, but it didn't last long before donations went up again.

Not only do the wealthy contribute an excess of money, but news sources go out of their way to inform the public of these donations. It's not done to shame the candidates who have accepted such donations, but to influence low-information voters on who they should be paying attention to rather than the candidate with the smaller budget but the better or more innovative ideas. Thus, it's another way of being led to where your vote should go.

All of these issues that plague the voting system can be avoided by appointing a president that is actually qualified to run the country. A lifelong leader with a good governing record should be appointed rather than being forced to run the humiliating gauntlet of being voted into office. No sane person would tell a firefighter how to fight a fire or a plumber how to fix a pipe if they have no knowledge of these things. Why tell a leader how to do their job if we're not ourselves professionals in the field? We cannot all work forty-hour plus jobs and be experts on the economy, foreign policy, or security matters as well. Americans are often ill-informed on voting issues simply because they don't hold political science degrees, or have no access to classified files relating to national security that hold information that can affect a decision.

President Meyers has done stellar work with both the economy and keeping the UCSA safe because he is a professional who understands the issues that we face. It is only responsible to let professionals do what is best for our families. If the government closed voting areas to keep us safe from Hariq Jihad this year, it is a testament to the governing that has so far kept us alive and prospering, and a move that should be considered permanent in the future. Onward to the next six years!

■ ■ ■

Jackson groaned and shut the webpage he was looking at. *The Union Standard Weekly Review* was delivered automatically via email to anyone working in the White House, and in general, he enjoyed reading the political tidbits and found some of the opinion columns entertaining. But this was something he wasn't exactly sure about. He understood, of course, why voting booths had been closed this year. With several direct threats made by Hariq Jihad, it was only sensible to close events that would involve large groups of people gathering together. Even baseball games and the like had been cancelled, it wasn't as though the voting booths were the only victims. But closing them in the long term? The thought made him distinctly uncomfortable, though the *Union Standard* writer had made some convincing arguments.

He put his feet up on his desk. He was early, for once, and had time to relax a little before getting down to the job. For a while now, he'd been in a background position, ever since the Vasquez shooting. But slowly he was getting back on his feet, no longer worried about holding or using a gun. In fact, in the two years or so since they'd moved to DC, he hadn't even had to draw his weapon, so safe and efficient was the president's security task force. On occasion, he made a trip to the shooting range, making sure that his skills were still up to scratch, as his secret service contract required him to. But on the whole, he was finding the work easy. A few years from now, he thought, happily smiling as he tipped back his desk chair, he'd be eligible for retirement with full military pension, and then he could get down to the serious business of living. Maybe even take up fishing.

The move to DC had worked out well for everyone. They decided on a small family house located in a nice cul de sac just outside of Alexandria, in the Virginia suburbs of DC. Courtney had loved the move, loved the house even more, and had devoted all her energies to decorating, making sure the girls were happy. She hosted dinner parties and PTA meetings along with all the other responsibilities of being a great mom.

Once again, Jackson thanked his lucky stars that he was the one that had saved Meyers's life. Without that stroke of luck, he'd never have had such a great job as this. When Meyers was in DC, Jackson worked his security detail, but the rest of the time he was free to do office work and spend time with his family. Just as Meyers had promised, there were no long trips, and certainly no foreign travel.

He still wondered from time to time about the assassination attempt. He felt partly culpable since he had trained Vasquez to be as good as he was. He felt that there was some blood on his hands.

He'd tried hard to remove the fond memories he had of Vasquez, though he wasn't always successful, and he hadn't forgotten his vow to confront Vasquez's parents, though he'd had no opportunity to do so thus far.

Working in the capital was nice. He sat around on top of the White House daily, surveying the grounds for any hidden targets. Most days he just watched the lawn through his scope and didn't worry. He knew that nothing bad was going to happen on his watch. People loved President Meyer and those that didn't were dealt with efficiently and quickly.

Times were different now. Some people were dissidents and didn't like the way things were going, but more and more of these people seemed to fade into the background. The only ones that remained vocal about it were the Apocalytes and secret operatives of the Hariq Jihad. This was because they worked together. He knew it, the press knew it, and everyone in his town knew it. Even the president himself had suggested it in the past—although there was no reason why anyone should worry now, because the president had it under control. He had signed a number of different laws making it easier for law enforcement to collect these people and bring them into the government to rehabilitate them.

The Apocalytes were an odd group. They were a cult—no one denied that—and they dedicated their lives to the old constitution of what had once been the United States. They based their whole lives on principles that were three hundred years old and were no longer applicable in 2078. They were a strange mix of politics and religion, with the basic tenet being that the Apocalypse or end of times was coming because the country had forgotten the basic rules of the original constitution. Odd, but there it was. There were enough of them that they had never all been successfully repressed, but so few that the public didn't take them seriously.

It was difficult for Apocalytes to find work, and there were a few communes scattered around, though more and more of these were being closed down. Somehow the propaganda, leaflets and old books beloved by the Apocalytes still managed to surface from time to time, ensnaring particularly the young.

Rehabilitating sounded easy enough, but all too often rehabilitation efforts didn't work. In these cases, rebels would eventually be sent off to a prison outside one of the major cities. When it worked, however, people came back. He sometimes felt a qualm of guilt about all this. He had occasionally seen a paper or a file where he couldn't quite grasp why someone had been arrested. Sometimes he wondered about those that weren't seen again. He'd heard rumors of course, but nothing definite.

He was certainly on the side of security, and backed the jailing of dissidents. But every now and again, he had to sign an order or look the other way as someone did something he didn't exactly approve of. Not that he thought everyone should have the right of free speech—that was ridiculous in this day and age. But there had to be a certain amount of dissension, of arguing, of differences of opinion, for a society to work, didn't there?

Jackson sighed again. It didn't do him any good to think about all this political shit. Besides, he was wasting his precious few moments of quiet before his work day began—time that would be better spent grabbing himself a coffee, he decided.

■ ■ ■

When Meyers was in town, Jackson's schedule was pretty set. He would wake at six in the morning to the piercing sound of his digital alarm clock. He might have used a cell phone to wake him, but he was constantly wary about keeping a phone by his bed, not wanting to become a slave to it. If someone really needed him, they would have access to his home phone number or even to his wife's number. Courtney kept her phone with her all the time, and in his opinion spent entirely too much time on it. Once awake, he would walk down to the kitchen and start brewing a cup of coffee in the single-serving coffee maker that Courtney had bought him for Christmas the year before.

Jackson liked his coffee tepid, a weird habit, but one he'd never broken. So while he waited, he'd go down to the basement and start his exercise routine. He started with full body stretches, making sure never to skip this step as it was what kept him so limber in his late thirties. He was still able to do a full split at his age. After the stretches, it was thirty push-ups, forty sit-ups and then a descending set of burpees, starting with ten and working his way down to one with one minute gaps between each set. He'd done the same routine for the last fifteen years and, not only did he still have his six-pack abs, he also had surprisingly low cholesterol, according to his doctor.

He didn't have to stay so fit anymore, of course, but he did enjoy being able to fit into his old Marine uniforms, some with a little room to spare. He certainly enjoyed feeling just that little bit superior to the other guys on his block, those ones with the beer bellies. That wasn't how he wanted to live his life. He knew because he'd heard his daughters' friends saying that he was considered attractive for his age, and that gave him a kick. Okay, so he shouldn't have been listening in, but he was a little protective of his girls. Every now and again he eavesdropped, just to make sure that nothing untoward was being discussed, like drugs, alcohol, or—God forbid—boys.

Jackson was able to make changes in the way he lived simply because he had plenty of time off when the president wasn't around, which was more often than he'd anticipated. On his days off, he'd start out with the same exercise routine and coffee but would also sit down to a good breakfast, before reading the news, then going for a run around the block.

On work days, on the other hand, after breakfast he'd shower, dress in the essential black suit, and head into work. During the trip to work, he'd listen to talk radio, sometimes switching it off in disgust if he heard something he didn't like about the country or the president, though that happened less and less often these days. Sometimes Vasquez's name would be mentioned, as he'd become somewhat of a poster boy for the terrorist movement—a man that no one could believe would be anything but patriotic. On these occasions, Jackson went to work a little more subdued.

He'd had the courage once or twice to send Vasquez's parents a check, though without an attached letter, hoping that it would cover some of their expenses. It seemed the least he could do since his family was comfortably taken care of, and he'd killed their main breadwinner. Each time he checked his account, the checks remained uncashed until they were void. He worried they might try to cash them after they expired, but as far as he knew, they never tried.

He wondered why things were the way they were—why people wouldn't accept help—although he knew he had no right to question it. When he had met Vasquez's parents, he remembered them being not poor but close to it. He knew that Vasquez regularly sent money home from his army paycheck, not just for his wife but also for his parents since they all lived in the same small house. He thought about how much these people must hate him to not be able to take his money when they probably desperately needed it. Although now that Mexico was in the Union, maybe the social safety net had been increased enough that the old couple could make ends meet without help. Who knew?

Jackson's day began quite normally, usually with him being debriefed by the men on the night shift. Generally he'd be told an awful lot of nothing, though if the night had happened to be one during which the president was hosting dignitaries, he might get some interesting stuff. There was nearly always a story about someone trying to have sex in one of the White House bathrooms on these occasions, not realizing how closely the president's home was guarded and watched. Sometimes it was even someone relatively famous. Whoever it was nearly always got caught, and while the guards found this hilarious, the culprits would need to be escorted out and reprimanded.

After that, he would go to his own office and plan out his day. This particular day was a Tuesday, which meant that he needed to be ready for a security drill that would happen at around 10:00 am. The drill was run every week at the exact same time. It was a realistic situation to keep the team well trained for any situation that the security trainers could dream up.

In Jackson's opinion, the likelihood of any of these various drill scenarios actually happening were so slim that the drills were tradition more than anything else. Tradition said that drills happened at 10:00 on Tuesdays, so they did. He'd once tried to move a drill to Wednesday due to a scheduling conflict and that hadn't gone over well.

Since he had a little time until the security drill, he relaxed outside of the Oval Office. There were a number of secret doors going in and out of the room, but Jackson preferred to stand guard outside the main door. He figured that if anyone was going to attempt to harm the president, then they would likely be stupid and/

or crazy, and in this case would probably just go in through the front door. Everyone else thought he was crazy himself for this, but since it was his call, he went ahead and did as he thought was right.

Jackson knew that if he had to plan an attack on President Meyers, then he would do it by ensuring that he took the path of least resistance. Since those secret doors were all barricaded and watched over like hawks, he figured that the easiest way to get in to the president's office would be to go through the front door.

Standing outside the front door, he would talk with Mitzy Fitzsimmons, the president's highly efficient secretary. She was in charge of handling the president's schedule and answering phone calls that came through the switchboard before they got to the president. While Jackson had never had cause to call the president after he moved to DC, he assumed that it must be incredibly annoying to do so, what with all the switchboards and secretaries you had to go through. Even if you got as far as Mitzy, she'd still need to check your name on a secure list of people that had telephone access to the president, take a message, or put you on hold. She was the last door that people had to unlock before getting to the president, and she was very good at her job.

"So, Mitzy, how's the family doing?"

"Not bad, Jackson, thank you for asking. And how about your girls? Ready to graduate yet?"

Mitzy was a real southern lady, and impeccably well mannered.

"Luckily we aren't quite there yet," answered Jackson. "She's certainly growing up, and starting to take an interest in politics too. You know how kids are with their fads and beliefs."

"Sure, I do know," said Mitzy, who was mother to three kids of her own. "Still convinced that the terrorists are going to walk through the front door?" she teased.

He grinned back at her. "Sure thing," he said. Then, more seriously, he added, "And if they do, I'll be right here waiting for them."

It was Mitzy's turn to grin now, knowing how seriously Jackson took his job.

Sometimes things brightened up, occasionally Jackson was on a security detail that involved overhearing conversations or negotiations, just as he had done in Mexico. At first he'd enjoyed these as a break in routine, though he'd never again witnessed Meyers look as intimidating as he had in Mexico. Here in Washington, Meyers seemed to get most of his wishes by charming people rather than by scaring them. Jackson got to watch a few pieces of history being made.

In the end, though, these negotiations were often boring and uninteresting. When Jackson did understand what was going on, he didn't always agree with the president's tactics. It wasn't his place to say anything, of course, but every now and again he felt uncomfortable on a gut level with something that he heard.

An example of this had occurred a couple of weeks ago, when Jackson had been asked to be on duty during a department of defense meeting at which the president would be addressing the cabinet. During the meeting, it had become increasingly clear that Meyers was pushing for something, and it took Jackson a while to figure out what.

"There is simply no more money in the budget for increased man power in the border areas," Meyer had said, half apologetically to the meeting. "And yes, I do realize that this puts us all in further danger, not to mention our families."

He had looked genuinely sorry about this, and it had confused Jackson. After all, the UCSA was economically sound, profits were increasing across the board, and there seemed to be plenty of money for other things. Besides, if it was necessary, then the defense department could surely move some man power away from the internal state borders and place more troops on the outside borders. The negotiations went back and forth with no solution in sight until Meyers picked up a piece of paper and surveyed it, then frowned as if thinking.

"It seems that a huge chunk of money is being spent on the trial process for dissidents," he remarked. "Could that money not be better used elsewhere?"

After that, it was just a matter of technicalities. Within an hour, the right to a fair hearing had been denied to all those accused of terrorist or counter-government activities. Jackson could see a point here, after all: terrorists shouldn't have the right to spend the public's tax money on trying to escape fair punishment. However, it grated on him. The whole point of the trial process was to ensure that the accused were actually guilty. In many cases, it was clear that the person on trial was culpable, but sometimes it wasn't—mistakes could be made. He knew that they could.

For the most part, Jackson tried to ensure that he wasn't present for these kinds of duties, using his natural charm to persuade other agents to go instead. Most of these agents welcomed the break from routine and were happy to accept.

In the meantime, Jackson put all he had heard out of his mind. The country was safe and prosperous, that was all that mattered. And he wasn't there to question the decisions of those more knowledgeable than himself. He was there to put his time in, get his pay check, and then head on home to his family—end of story.

8

THE THIRD YEAR

November 2nd, 2078
Washington DC, UCSA
Article Originally Published in the *National UCSA Tribune*, Reused with Permission

Polls Once More to Be Closed
James Allen, News Editor

For a third year in a row, polling places are to be closed on November 2nd due to an increased security threat from Hariq Jihad. President Meyers announced the closures at a press conference held on the White House lawn late yesterday afternoon. He expressed his displeasure with having to bow to the pressures placed on him by the terrorist organization but admitted that there was little else that could be done. The safety of the general populace is his "absolute priority above all else." The announcement was met with approval across the board and seen as just one more piece of evidence that the president is still a man of the people and for the people. It will be no hardship to retain the services of Meyers for another year until Election Day 2079.

■ ■ ■

Jackson barely even noticed the article as he checked his morning email. He was too busy bounding up the stairs, energized after his morning workout and ready to get started with his day. A few minutes later, a sense of unease came over him.

"Hey, hun," he shouted to Courtney. "I keep feeling like there's somewhere I'm supposed to go today, but I can't remember where it is. Did you ask me to go anywhere for you today?"

He was in the middle of shaving. He'd always been clean shaven, and now it was regulation anyway. Similar to when he was a Marine: either he was clean shaven or he would reap the punishment of his superiors. The most he was allowed to have was a moustache, but most people didn't bother with those anymore; they'd fallen out of fashion.

"I don't think so, honey," came Courtney's voice from the walk-in closet where she was choosing her outfit for the day. "But you should ask the girls. Maybe they asked you to do something for them?"

Jackson splashed water on his face and wiped off the remainder of his shaving cream before he walked back into the bedroom. He opened the door a few inches and stuck his head out to yell to the girls, mindful of the fact that he was only in his underwear.

"MacKenzie, Maya, did either of you ask me to do something for you this morning? I keep thinking I've forgotten something important!"

He was aware of how odd the question sounded, but he really had a deep-seated feeling of something forgotten, something very important.

"No, Daddy," chorused the girls from their respective rooms.

"Alright then. Thanks," he answered. "If you guys hurry up, I can take you to school," he said, as he closed the door.

"I'm missing something for sure," he said to Courtney who was starting to get dressed. "What day is it today?"

She thought for a second before replying, "November second, I think." Then she went back to battling with a pair of tights that she was trying to get on without lying on the bed with her legs in the air.

"What usually happens on the second of November?" Jackson said, half to himself. "Let's see, yesterday was…"

"Monday," said Courtney jokingly as she jumped up and down squeezing into her tights, finally.

"So it's Tuesday," Jackson said, ignoring her sarcasm. "What the hell do I have to do on a Tuesday that's so important?"

Courtney picked up the remote and switched the television in their room on before going to get another pair of tights. The set flickered on to the National News Network.

A voice from the screen said:

"… and today's high will be fifty degrees, which will be a welcome break from this cold morning air. And now on to the traffic report with Wanda Ferrera. So tell us, Wanda, how is the commute into DC this morning?"

"Can you turn it up please?" said Jackson to Courtney, who was rummaging through a drawer, remote still in her hand. "I really need to hear the traffic."

The voice of Wanda Ferrera slowly got louder as she spoke on the screen.

"Well, traffic into DC is looking relatively good for this Tuesday morning, the first Tuesday of November..." The announcer paused for a second, and then said, "And why do I feel like today is a very important day?"

"See, Court, it's not just me," Jackson said. "There is something important today."

Courtney turned her attention to the TV as the weather announcer and the traffic adviser continued to go back and forth, trying to figure out the significance of the day. As Courtney was about to turn away, the television went quiet, hummed, and then a new voice was heard—one that was distorted, almost like the disguised voice of a confidential informants.

"Citizens of the UCSA, wake up!" said the voice. "You are being lied to!"

Jackson rolled his eyes. "Jesus, turn this crap off, Courtney. Change the channel or something."

Courtney sat on the edge of the bed and pressed the channel button on the remote, but though the channel number in the top corner of the set changed, the voice and its message did not. The voice was on every single channel, and Jackson couldn't help but hear what it was saying.

"We are the Apocalytes. We have come to tell you of the world that once was. Years ago this day, November second, would have been Election Day. This is the day when you should be voting for your president. The day when you should be exercising your democratic rights, but you are not. You are being lied to. Things are not the way they seem. Where have your friends disappeared to? Why is military spending so high when we are not at war with anyone? And where is this Hariq Jihad that is to be so feared? Citizens rise up, you can take this country back..."

The interruption itself was then interrupted, the distorted voice fading out, drowned by the emergency broadcast signal, and then replaced by a far more familiar voice. As the loud, piercing electronic beep was silenced, the voice of Braddock Smith, press secretary to President Meyers, could be heard. His face slowly came on the screen, his familiar profile comforting after the sudden intermission. Smith was standing in front of the presidential seal, one that had been redesigned since the country had become the UCSA. Gone was the traditional eagle, replaced instead by a far more regal-looking griffin.

"Greetings, citizens of this great nation," said Smith, his voice authoritarian. "In an unprecedented move, the Apocalytes have hijacked national television feeds nationwide. However, do not fear. This cyber-terrorism will not be taken lightly and will not go unpunished. The president had vowed to make it a priority of his administration to rid the country of these kinds of dissenters. As always, if you see something, say something. You can call the national police hotline any time at 1-855..."

The voice trailed off as Courtney turned down the volume on the set. Jackson was no longer listening anyway, as he was much more focused on getting himself out of the house. Once he arrived at work, he could find out what was going on.

"I wonder, Ant," Courtney said, still sitting on the edge of the bed and watching him frantically getting dressed. "I wonder why we don't have elections anymore. Lord knows, I don't miss all the political ads, but we really should have had an election by now, shouldn't we?"

Just why had they stopped having elections?, Jackson wondered. Sure, there was all that confusion after the attempt on Meyers's life, but they should have been able to get the system fixed by now, he thought. However, he quickly dismissed the thought, as he was loyal to his government. Besides, all doubts did was make you more likely to become an extremist.

"I don't know, honey," he said, knotting his tie. "It's probably because we've got a lot of terrorists in this country. Can't give them a chance to destroy the government from within."

"I guess," she said, running her fingers through her long, dark hair and twisting it into a bun. "Don't worry about the kids, Ant. I'll get them to school."

He grinned at her in relief. He'd forgotten that he'd only just promised the girls he'd take them to school, just moments ago. Then he swooped in to drop a kiss on her cheek, rushed out of the bedroom, yelled goodbye to the girls as he was running down the stairs, and was in his car a moment later. Normally, he turned the auto-drive on the car off as he preferred to be in control. Today, though, he let it drive him all the way to work because he had a lot to think about.

Elections—he'd heard the opinion that the entire game of having elections was foolishness, though he'd given the matter little thought himself. It was true that the same people tended to win anyway, and more importantly these days, election season was typically used by the Hariq Jihad to attempt to further their own agenda. According to security reports, the group were often caught trying to carry out terrorist actions in order to thwart the rule of law and to get their operatives elected into government. In fact, as Jackson knew, it had happened once or twice that a senator or congressman had to be forcibly removed from office. These individuals were confirmed by sources close to the government to have been elected due only to hacking and other subversive actions committed by the Hariq Jihad.

So the people were forced to give up the idea of presidential and congressional elections in order to avoid the mechanizations of the Hariq Jihad. So what?, Jackson thought, it was better to be safe than sorry. They could all agree on that, couldn't they?

Anyway, as far as he could see, most people were happy with the way things had turned out, just like Courtney had said. They didn't have to deal with the endless, boring cycle of presidential politics anymore. There was one president, each state had their own federal representative, and that was all there was. If someone died or was removed from office for whatever reason, then a replacement was appointed by the Governor of the state or by the President, depending on that individual's role in the government. Besides, it wasn't as if democracy had gone out the window. There were still local and state elections. Mayors and city council members were still elected by the people. It was simply the more skilled roles that were appointed and only when needed. That seemed to be a fair compromise, at least, Jackson reasoned.

There wasn't a reason to bother people with all this stuff for the time being, and he couldn't see what the point of the Apocalytes' message had been, other than to create trouble. Of course, at some point the government was going to have to do something to ensure that local elections were not a place where the Hariq Jihad could get a foothold. As everyone knew from the incident with Vasquez, even a small incursion from the Jihadists could easily create an international incident. The president would often spend time meeting with local and state government officials, so it only made sense for security services to keep an eye on local elections. Of course it was necessary to ensure that only a certain kind of person could make changes in government.

In Jackson's opinion, the Apocalytes worried too much about this great society of the past and the founding fathers, all of which were irrelevant now. He believed in democracy, of course he did, but not in the chaotic democracy of the past. The Apocalytes were absolutely insane, and there was no way that people such as them, to make a good example, should be allowed to make changes to the government.

Certainly, Jackson thought as his car slowed for a red light, that was why there were so many different and complicated rules about voting. First a family had to be in good standing with the government, meaning that they could never have been suspected of terrorism or sympathy for the terrorist cause. This automatically made a large number of people ineligible to vote, since the rule applied to anyone within two generations either side of the offending family member. Many young, new voters were automatically eliminated from the voting pool anyway, since it was a rare teenager these days that didn't at least flirt with the ideas of the Apocalytes. Generally this was just a passing phase, and Jackson wasn't sure that these people should be ineligible to vote, but he recognized that it would be difficult to distinguish between those with a passing infatuation versus those that had truly believed.

Unpaid tickets or disregarded court summonses were another reason that people were not allowed to vote. You could not owe any money to the government—local or federal. This was in order to encourage prompt payment, which made sense to Jackson. You could get tickets for pretty much anything these days, but paying them was still important, and preventing such debtors from voting in local elections was surprisingly effective.

Anyway, the upshot of all this was that people tended to just stay home when it came to local elections. There was little point in bothering to vote when everything was so well taken care of by the government anyway. The unemployed were given work, the homeless given homes, and the sick had full access to Government Health Services. Why should there be discontent? Sure, there was less free movement, but for most, that was a small price to pay for complete security. More often, people were simply relieved that there was no pressure to have the responsibility of voting for leaders. Voting was the old model, Jackson thought, and not one that was especially applicable anymore. It was something that the Apocalytes might want, but the general population? Nah, they just weren't that bothered.

His car made its way onto the small side street that would eventually curve around and give him access to the underground parking lot by the White House. The thing that still bothered him was what had happened this morning. The Apocalytes were fools, outdated, living in the past—a cult with ridiculous ideas. So why were they still around? Why hadn't they just fizzled out like all the other protest groups had over the years?

He knew that most other citizens felt the same way as he did about the Apocalytes. It was hard to figure out why anyone would look at a country that could provide its citizens with almost everything they needed and wonder where the nation got the right to give the citizenry such riches. Since the government kept most things in tip-top shape and there was so little for people to complain about, most sensible citizens wouldn't even think about joining the Apocalytes. No, the Apocalytes didn't prey on normal people; instead, they riled up the disenchanted and bored youth, giving them a purpose in a society that barely had anything for them to rebel against.

Maybe that was part of the price, he mused as he slid into the curve that would take him into the parking lot. Meyers had created such a perfect, vanilla world that a certain kind of person had to join up with the Apocalytes in order to experience any kind of thrill. Rebellion—an age-old problem. He tried to remember rebelling himself, but got only as far as a cigarette he'd once tried at fourteen before running out of examples. When you were busting your ass to get food on the table, there wasn't much time for rebellion. Or maybe he just wasn't the rebellious type.

What these fools—these rebel Apocalytes—forgot was the most important thing. Since the advent of the new laws, since the founding of the UCSA, there had not been a single successful attack inside the country. While you might not like not being able to hop over to Florida for some sunshine, who wanted to live a life scurrying around in fear?

Tens of thousands of people had died in the bombings of 2051. The death toll had been so high that the memorial couldn't include the names of everyone that had perished on that day. Individual towns and cities had their own memorials, of course, but one, national memorial? Impossible.

This was not to be allowed to happen again. Jackson might not himself always feel comfortable with some of the more draconian measures the government took, but he always understood what was happening and why. The fact was that all of these measures still made the UCSA a pleasant, prosperous country to live in. Things could be much, much worse. His car signaled that he needed to take over parking. He pulled into his designated parking space and commanded the car to turn off before reaching over to grab his jacket from the passenger seat. Yes, that was what fools like the Apocalytes didn't get. Things could be far worse.

9

November 5th, 2078
Alexandria, Virginia, UCSA

Jackson woke up soaked in sweat. His eyes flashed open, taking a second to adjust to the faintly lit darkness, and then he quickly scanned the room and realized where he was. He'd almost forgotten that he was at home with his wife and children. He'd thought for a brief and horrifying moment that he was back in Mexico.

It had been happening for a while now—a few months. It was stress, he told himself, that had triggered the night terrors, but now he wasn't so sure. It was always a variation of the same horrible event. He always felt the same helplessness, the same paralysis, and the same black hole of fear.

It was mid-afternoon in Mexico. In his dream, for whatever reason, everything was in a deep brown hue, as if everything had been coated with the same brown dust that covered the terrain of the country. The dust that got into his rifle, stuck between his toes, and invaded his ears and eyes. Over and over again, the dream would run in a circle, stopping only when he awoke. He would see himself there all over again, watching himself but being completely unable to affect the action, unable to change the path that his dream-self followed.

He'd dream that he was talking to Vasquez, his angel face shining, worried and yet excited about what he was going to do. He would beg and plead with Vasquez to stop, to think about what he was doing. He would stand over Vasquez, who was already in position, hunched over his rifle, ready to take a shot. He would scream at him, jostle, punch and strangle him, and eventually shoot him to try make him stop, but it never worked. Nothing ever stopped Vasquez from taking the shot, wounding Meyers and killing Espinoza. Even if he had to rise, zombie-like, from the ground, his face hanging off from the bullet Jackson had drilled into his brain, Vaszquez still made the shot.

There was nothing that would prevent the events of the dream from unfolding. It was not every night; somehow that would have been better, expected even. Instead he could go for a week without one, and then have it three nights in a row, always taking him by surprise, terrifying him more simply because he didn't expect to dream tonight. In the back of his mind lurked an ugly possibility: this could be something more serious, like post- traumatic stress disorder. It could be he was just going crazy. He knew that seeking any kind of help would mean immediate removal from his detail on presidential security. That was something that he wouldn't risk; he wasn't going to lose this job and all the benefits attached.

So there was little he could do, other than deal with the dreams as best as he could. He kept them from Courtney and the kids, trying to explain things away, never letting anyone know exactly what was wrong. This led to him often sleeping on the couch, afraid to wake Courtney with his nightmares. When the kids came in to watch TV, cereal in hand, he had to explain that he'd fallen asleep watching TV, or that mommy snored too loud, which made MacKenzie giggle. He always deflected the questions, never letting on that he was suffering from these night terrors.

He secretly read articles about PTSD and dealing with the disorder, carefully covering his tracks by deleting his internet history, and leaving magazines and journals in the car where no one would find them. He read story after story of military men and women, tales of how even the smallest of events that happened in the heat of battle could make it hard when they returned home. Each found different ways of dealing with their traumatic event. Some of them told stories of going to the homes of the families of their fallen comrades, of giving apologies to these families for being unable to save their son or daughter from enemy fire. This struck a chord with Jackson.

Others found great relief in writing letters to the dead, or to the enemy that had caused the trauma. Some were doing nothing but going out into the middle of the woods once in a while and yelling curse words at the top of their lungs, getting out all the frustration, anger and fear that had built up. For once, Jackson grinned at the picture of a presidential secret service agent being caught yelling swear words in his back yard, but in his heart he knew it wasn't really funny.

He read that it wasn't his fault, that his mental and physical reactions weren't his to take the blame for. He knew this in his head, but getting his heart and mind to believe it was another matter.

As often as he could, he'd sit at the breakfast table, drinking coffee with Courtney and watching the kids eat their sugary cereal that they could have only on Saturdays. He thought how lucky he was, despite the nightmares, despite his problems. One morning, a box of Lucky Charms half-emptied into her bowl, MacKenzie looked up at him and said, "Dad?"

"Yes, sweetie?"

"How come you always sleep in the living room?" she hardly looked up from shoveling spoonfuls of marshmallowy goodness into her mouth.

"I don't always sleep in the living room," he said, rolling his eyes at Courtney in fake surprise at the weird things that kids say.

"Yes you do," said MacKenzie, another spoon of cereal poised before her mouth. "You sleep in there all the time."

Jackson shrugged, but noticed that Courtney was looking at him strangely, her brow furrowed. "Sometimes, I wake up at night and can't sleep so I go to the living room and watch TV so I don't wake up Mom, and then I fall asleep."

Everyone seemed satisfied with the answer, and then they were distracted by the cat knocking over a carton of juice, so he was off the hook. He just didn't want anyone to hear him crying in the night, waking up and not knowing what to do next, thinking that he was still back there in Mexico.

He'd tried everything he could think of to sleep through the night. He'd even tried yoga, sneaking down to the basement before bed. He'd felt weird enough but had given it a try anyway. Yoga, he thought, was for New York City hipsters, not for a tough-as-nails Marine. It had been recommended in an article he'd read, so he thought it worth a try. It had been one of the more interesting, as he would put it, ways of attempting to overcome his trauma. He moved, twisting and turning this way and that in an attempt to make some kind of connection with inner peace and joy, trying with all his might to see some results. Though he undeniably felt more relaxed, the exercises did nothing for his mind. He slept no more soundly after yoga than he did any other night and could see no relationship between the dreams and his exercise. He continued trying until he hurt himself—a pulled muscle in his back and a month of painkillers dissuaded him from doing any more yoga.

After yoga, he went to the shooting range as a way to relieve himself of his nightly visits from his personal demons. After returning from the military he'd retired his service weapons, using nothing other than his standard-issue pistol. He could shoot with the pistol on the range, but couldn't bring himself to look at, let alone touch, any rifle, despite the fact that they had once felt like an extension of his body. Pressure came from an unlikely source: MacKenzie was going through a stage where she was not only a tomboy but also into all things survivalist. While camping was fine, she was on his case, begging and pleading for her daddy to take her hunting like some of the boys in her class at school did with their fathers.

She'd always call him 'daddy' when she wanted something. Normally, she was of the age now where 'dad' was the word. Therefore, he knew that when he heard 'daddy,' something was up. He didn't even want to imagine what she wanted if she ever called him 'father.'

"Daddy, when do you think we can go hunting?"

"It's not the right season for it now, Macky."

He'd always call her Macky when she called him daddy. It was a little joke that he'd found for himself and hoped he wouldn't have to explain to her and show his age.

"Last season you said next season, and this season you say not now," she whined. "It's not fair, you never want to do the things I want to do."

It pissed him off a little when she whined—both girls had been brought up not to—but he bit his tongue, knowing that he was the one at fault here.

"I'd do it," he said. "But you always forget to ask until after the season's done. Next time."

So it went on and on. She had this idea in her head and would not let it go. Every time she asked, he'd stall with the season excuse, dreading the time when she got wise to the tactic and actually looked up when the seasons were for herself. Every time she asked, he'd resolve that he was going to do something about the fear inside him, not just because of the dreams, but for his little girl. Each time, he chickened out.

The dreams kept coming, consistently getting worse and appearing more realistic. He was desperate. All he wanted was a solution, and if a website had suggested that he eat snails while swimming the Potomac, he'd have done it. He needed to do something and take back control of his life. So far this hadn't affected his work, other than a few yawns, but at some point it was going to, and it was certainly already affecting his family. He had to do something.

Jackson was a brave man, that he knew, but the decision to take out the black Remmington Bolt-Action rifle that his father had presented him with for his twelfth birthday was one of the bravest things he'd ever had to do. He had to muster up all his courage even to think about it.

The rifle had been one of the weapons that he had not been able to bring himself to use again, but that he also couldn't fathom getting rid of. It was one of the only things he could remember his father giving him, so it was valuable for sentimental reasons. He kept it in the back of his closet inside a locked gun safe that only he and Courtney had keys to. Gun safety was paramount in his house, even if he wasn't planning on using the weapons. As the kids got older, he'd spoken to them about what was in the room, and both were aware of the dangers and knew why the door was locked. He trusted them to use their common sense.

He sighed as he put the key into the door, not quite able to bring himself to turn it. Things hadn't always been like this, he reminded himself. He hadn't always had the dreams. In fact, he couldn't really figure out when exactly they'd started, when all this had begun. It had seemed to happen slowly at first, flinching at loud noises. Then he couldn't stay asleep, not that he'd remember the nightmares vividly, except those that involved Vasquez. He'd wake at three or four in the morning and be filled with a paralyzing sense of dread with no idea why—a dread that he'd never felt before.

Maybe, he thought as he turned the key and heard it click, maybe a way to stop all this would be to get back on the horse. If he could get used to his rifle, if he could take his daughter out hunting, then he could go back to being normal. Perhaps he needed to be able to use his rifle to remind himself that he wasn't powerless, and that he could protect himself and everyone else. That might be the feeling that he had forgotten, that power that kept all the bad things, the feeling of impending doom, in check. He had to muscle up and get in there.

He opened the door and took a deep breath, unable to believe that the thought of a gun could affect him this way. He was going to do this. He started slowly at first, by cracking open the door of the safe and looking in at the rifle, propped up against the wall of the safe in the far right corner. He stared at it for ten minutes, trying to calm his breathing. Then he moved to touch it, starting with stroking the cool metal body, and working his way up to holding it, feeling its weight in his hands. After a couple of weeks, he managed to take the rifle down to the range and shoot it, his heart beating wildly. His fear of rifles left him with that first shot, and he confirmed that he still had kept his skill. That night he had another nightmare. Being able to use his rifle had nothing to do with it. He needed to try to find another solution.

Then came the night when his secret was blown. For some reason, he didn't wake up in time. He had slept badly the previous night and had figured he would be safe enough this night, so he'd stayed in bed sleeping next to Courtney. When he woke up shouting, she was immediately cradling him.

"What is it? What's wrong, Ant?" she crooned, in the same way she'd talked to the girls when they were little and had had bad dreams.

For a minute or so, he'd been unable to articulate what had happened, but in the end, in his sleep deprived and vulnerable state, in the dark of the bedroom, he'd told her. He'd told her everything, the words slipping out without him realizing what he was saying. She held him for the rest of the night and he slept soundly, comforted by her arms, the weight on his chest lessened simply by sharing his secret with her.

Courtney had worked in an office as an office manager before she had Maya. She had started as an administrator and filer but had proven to be great at her job, eventually making her way to managing the office. She had stopped working to take care of their daughter, and then a second daughter came along. Jackson had figured that if his wife wanted to stay home, then she should stay home. He'd never asked her to work, and in truth was happy that his daughters had a mother that wanted to be with them and care for them.

In the years since Maya's, and then MacKenzie's, birth, Courtney had never once expressed a word of regret about being a stay-at-home mom. She loved staying with her kids and teaching them how to grow up into responsible, loving and caring adults. She missed the challenges of work, although the family's finances meant there was no need for a second income. As the girls grew up, her constant presence at home was security for them, but she could feel that it was also starting to be a little annoying. Feeling that though she wanted to be there for them, she was also somewhat in their way.

She decided that she wanted to go back to work part-time. The problem now was that she lacked confidence after not working for so long. If she could rise to the challenge of helping her husband, she'd rise to the challenge of job hunting, she'd thought. She wanted to help Jackson as she knew that he couldn't ask for professional help.

She was busy at home cooking and cleaning but still had plenty of time to take care of the things that she wanted. After Jackson had clued her in to his problem, she worked on it every afternoon. She spent hours researching PTSD, reading everything from scientific journal articles to personal anecdotes. Jackson, she knew, wouldn't appreciate what she was doing. He thought it was his job to take care of the problem, but she reminded herself that she was doing it for him, for herself, and for their family. She just wanted her husband to have a good night's sleep.

Being able to look at things more objectively than Jackson gave her an edge. After days of research, she read an article about how a man had been able to make peace with the traumatic incident that he had experienced, in his case being unable to stop one of his friends being killed on the battle field. The man had been wrought with guilt and despair over being unable to save his friend from enemy fire, wondering why he had lived when his friend had died. He couldn't sleep, couldn't work, and had experienced all the same PTSD signs that Jackson had. He had solved this by taking a trip to his comrade's family home to meet with his parents. This gave her an idea.

"You need to go to Mexico," she told Jackson as soon as the girls were in bed.

They were sitting on the deck enjoying a quiet glass of wine. Jackson gave no sign that he had thought about this solution for a long time, that he'd been putting it off because he was afraid, but that he'd come to the same conclusion as she had. Before he'd wanted to make amends, do what was right, but now it had become a question of his own sanity, and the issue was more pressing.

"You need to make peace with Vasquez's family," Courtney said, reaching out to take his hand.

He nodded, staying silent. She was right, he knew. Hopefully they weren't going to hate him too much, him, the man that had killed their son. Maybe they'd be able to see reason, maybe recognize that he'd had no choice. After all, their son had tried to kill Meyers.

"Yes," he said, finally. "Yes, I do."

He knew that once she had an idea in her head she'd never let it go, and didn't want to hash through the idea at all. She was right, he knew it, and that was that. He determined to arrange his trip as soon as possible. He needed to see his family.

10

THE VISIT

November 28th, 2078
Palmer International Airport, Washington DC, UCSA
Article Originally Published in the *Mexico Register*,
Reused with Permission
Death of the Cartels: The End of an Era
Luiz Valez Escada, Crime Editor

The Mexican cartels have long been at odds with the United Continental States of America, first within Mexico and the NAU, and later within the UCSA itself, but it looks as though their reign of terror may be coming to an end. For over a quarter of a century, cartels have been a significant crime organization in the southern area of the nation, but the UCSA has made great strides in eradicating these unlawful groups. This action is cause for celebration and gratitude.

While many in the country do not see the immediate effects of the removal of the cartels, the southern portion of our great union was terrorized by these unlawful Latino groups for years before the rule of President Meyers began took action. As an example, cartels would frequently transport hard-working but illegal immigrants from Central America into the union, passing them through legal immigration check points or smuggling them through. They charged exorbitant prices for such transport, sometimes robbing and killing those under their care.

People were the only products moved by the cartels across the border after the federal legalization of marijuana. Before, the cartels were frontrunners in drug smuggling. Occasionally contraband would be caught at border check points, but a significant amount of product would make it inside the union, resulting in the kind of addiction and crime problems that legalization has now eradicated.

Cartels also frequently profited from the kidnapping and ransoming of American citizens. For decades, Mexico City and Phoenix, Arizona topped the list of cities with the most kidnappings in the union. Some victims were fortunate enough to have family members able to pay such ransoms, but many more could not pay the cartels and ended up in sex slavery.

More recently, cartels have been heavily implicated in the Hariq Jihad movement, with strong connections found between the groups. The transportation and smuggling systems established by the cartels have been used to move terrorists in and out of the UCSA. Hariq Jihad has wealthy supporters, and cartels gladly take their money, hiding terrorists among the regular immigrants heading north.

Of course, the merger of Mexico with the North American Union to form the United Continental States of America was seen by the cartels as a God send, as people needed to be moved from Guatemala to Mexico, rather than up into what had been the NAU, a significantly easier trip than ever before. This was aided by the fact that Guatemala has a large Muslim population after mass migrations earlier this century following wars in the Middle East. Therefore, support for Hariq Jihad south of the UCSA border is strong. Current thinking is that this Central American move of Muslims was due to the easy implementation of Sharia law in these impoverished countries, in stark contrast to the long and bloody process undertaken to implement Sharia law in countries such as France. In addition, of course, the cartels and Hariq Jihad have a vested interest in destabilizing the old NAU borders. Cartels supply the terrorist organization with resources and offer non-terrorist Muslims with basic living supplies at a price, a symbiosis of danger for the northern areas.

One can look at these facts and wonder how the United Continental States of America is prospering as it currently is. However, under the direction of President Meyers, the UCSA military has made serious headway in containing and reducing the threat of the Mexican cartels and Hariq Jihad, with the invaluable help of Regional Vice President Menendez.

The truth is that the merger of Mexico and the NAU was not as positive for the cartels as they first thought. Once the two nations became the UCSA, the full strength of combined military forces were able to penetrate cartel-held areas in the south of Mexico and flush out many of their members. While there still may be some small presence in the Mexico region, it is a marginalized one at best. The cartels also have apparent financial problems due to this show of strength. Furthermore, Mexicans are now citizens of the UCSA, lessening the number of individuals trying to leave Mexico.

A further blow to the cartels was the protection offered to the average Mexican citizen by the UCSA forces. With the UCSA forces in place, citizens began to take a stand and even cooperate with authorities, giving valuable information and revealing cartel safe houses. With President Meyers came the promise of bringing an end to corrupt government officials that accepted bribes and looked the other way when it came to the criminal element.

Mexico has become a far safer and more prosperous region under the UCSA, a fact that we can all be thankful for. However, there is still work to be done. Terrorists still attempt to cross the Guatemalan border, and Mexican cartels still help them. There have also been signs of Apocalytes acting in the area. We must be vigilant with our borders, as well as between our borders, though monitoring travel between the states makes safe passage for both terrorists and the cartels incredibly difficult. Despite these small issues, it does appear that we are witnessing the dying days of the cartels. And it will be a death that none of us grieve.

■ ■ ■

Not a bad thing, Jackson thought, as he closed the article. Defeating the cartels must have taken immense military force, and he wondered how the snipers he had trained had fared in these battles.

His leg bounced up and down of its own accord as he sat in the airport lounge. He'd already read through the Mexican news articles on his tablet as well as three others he had downloaded. He'd been desperately early, but that was the nerves. It was all nerves. Ever since he'd taken that flight home from Mexico, he'd feared going back. He couldn't take sleeping pills as he wanted to have his wits about him. President Meyers made it easier for him to fly than it was to drive, and he needed to do this. He needed to get his family and his sanity back, and that meant he had to get on this damn flight. His mouth was a little dry and he just wanted to have the whole thing over with.

He sat and sat, waiting for the plane to board, nervous, worried, and sick over what was going to happen next. He'd vowed never to go back there, and yet here he was. He hated it when life didn't go as planned. Voices caught his attention, and he settled his eyes on the couple arguing two rows in front of him.

They were a couple of kids, at least to his eyes, who couldn't have been more than twenty. It was getting harder for him to judge age as he got older. He imagined that they must have gotten married right out of college, maybe even during college. While they were trying to have their angry conversation as quietly as possible, he could overhear their argument and knew exactly what they were talking about.

They both looked just as nervous as Jackson imagined he did, maybe more, and the girl looked upset. She was around average height, with dark brown hair that was pressed straight and pushed back off her forehead with a white and blue headband. They looked like they were dressed for a weekend trip, possibly a pleasure trip to Cancun. He wondered how long they'd had to wait for permission to travel; this might be their honeymoon. It struck him as odd that they had so much luggage for a vacation.

He could hear bits and pieces of their conversation, some parts disappearing as people closer to him spoke. He picked up a good amount of it, though. He wasn't exactly trying to eavesdrop, but he'd read through all the news articles that he could and was bored with the mobile games he had on his phone. He sat and listened, feeling slightly guilty, as he waited for boarding.

"I told you not to bring it," the boy said, in a hushed voice.

"But it was my mother's," she whispered back.

"Attention: will Jasmine Plano please come to the courtesy counter?" added the announcement system.

"...caught," was the only word that Jackson got from whatever had just been said.

The boy's voice was low but firm, and he looked around himself constantly as if to reassure himself that no one was looking. Jackson wasn't really looking at them but had been glancing occasionally. He kept his hands folded in his lap, looking up at the ceiling for the most part. He'd been attempting to count how many holes the speaker on the ceiling had, but he'd get to around fifteen and need to start all over. It was a way to spend the time, and he'd had plenty of practice of sitting around and waiting in the military. Military life wasn't all fighting and action. In fact, it was the minimum of fighting and action—a hurry-up-and-wait life.

"So you don't want me to have something to remember her by?" the girl was saying.

"It's not that, it's just..."—the boy's voice became very quiet, so that Jackson could barely make out what he was saying—"...it's dangerous."

Jackson found his interest distinctly piqued. Now what could these two possibly be doing in Mexico that was dangerous? There was only one possible thing that he could think of, and it made him sad. The cartels didn't only take money to get people into the UCSA, they took money to get people out as well—people who didn't love the country as much as Jackson himself did. These folks thought they could live a better life outside of the strict rules and governing of the UCSA. Fools, in Jackson's opinion, but there were others like them. He didn't understand it.

He sighed inwardly. They'd both likely die out there in the wilderness with the untrustworthy coyotes of the cartels. He was torn. If he reported them, as he knew he should, they'd end up in a detention center and maybe even in one of the jails for dissenters. If he didn't report them, then they'd probably end up at the least being taken advantage of by the cartels and at the worst, dead and rotting out in the desert.

He looked at the girl and felt sorry for her. She made him think of his own daughters, and he'd do anything to keep them out of the detention centers, even though he loved his own country. He hoped for their sake that they didn't meet a bad fate and realized that he'd keep his mouth shut. He would have to let them try for it; it was their decision, after all. Even though he didn't agree with what they were doing, the UCSA was probably better off without people who didn't fully support her leaders. Would Guatemala or Belize be better?, he wondered. Only time would tell. But he wouldn't be the guy to turn them in.

Thinking and listening in had given him a few minutes of distraction that he was happy for. He didn't really want to think about what was going to happen when he got to Mexico, though he knew he should. He was happy for the smallest of distractions that allowed him to procrastinate.

They continued to fight, but having figured out their mystery and deciding on a course of action, Jackson was no longer interested. He really should try and plan out this trip. An announcement screeched overhead. He needed to figure out what he was going to say and do. Surely the Vasquez's would be angry with him, no matter how right his actions had been. He was certain that he had done the right thing by killing Vasquez, as it had been the only thing he could do in order to save Meyers. He hadn't wanted to shoot the guy, but he'd been about to take another shot at the president, Jackson was sure of it, so if he hadn't shot when he did, then Vasquez could well have killed Meyers. He reminded himself of these facts repeatedly, but still found that he was racked by guilt about what had transpired on that hot, sweaty day.

He tried to imagine himself getting off the airplane in Mexico City, walking through things logically, step by step. He would go down to baggage claim and wait until his bag came towards him, inevitably one of the last on the conveyor belt. Then he would go outside and find a taxi to take him to the hotel. Or should he go straight to the Vasquez's home? Whichever he decided on, he was still going to be back at home in DC the next day.

Taking the trip, while not as difficult as it would be for most people, had still been an inconvenience. He'd had to request travel documents so that he could travel across the country, and then explain to the president why he was going there. Once the president heard how Anthony's guilt was eating him alive, he'd understood and pushed everything through.

Travel restrictions had become tighter since he'd moved to Washington, and in order to get the travel papers, or the TR-4986 as they kept calling it in the office, he would've normally had to go to the travel department. He was required to bring letters of recommendation from two people who knew him but weren't related to him. There were also the documents that he would've had to provide to prove the he didn't have any tickets, violations or any other difficulties with any local, state or federal government agency. Just getting all the papers that proved he had a clean slate was tough enough, but the fees required to get them all as quickly as he needed them were extortionate. He briefly thought that if the remainder of the cartels were having money problems, maybe they should consider going into bureaucracy rather than crime.

When Courtney decided something had to be done, it had to be done right away, otherwise she'd nag his ear off about it until she got her way. He'd needed to get this over and done with as fast as possible for himself as well. Fast tracking his vacation time was a nightmare made easier by the fact that President Meyers was leaving DC and didn't need Jackson's protection. In the end, everything had fallen into place perfectly for him.

If this was what was necessary to get rid of these damn nightmares and to get his life and sanity back, then he was just going to have to do it. His leg started bouncing up and down again, and his backside started to go numb from the hard metal chair he was sitting in.

"Attention: Flight number 476 to Mexico City is now open for boarding at gate B12," said the harsh female voice over the announcement system.

About time, Jackson thought. He stood up and stretched one final time before getting on the plane. As he walked through the jet bridge connecting the plane to the boarding gate he came to a decision. He would go to his hotel first before going to see the Vasquez family. It would be weird for him to be standing there with luggage in hand asking forgiveness from the parents of the man he had killed.

Mexico City, UCSA

It wasn't the heat that was unbearable this time of year in Mexico City. The warmth was nice after the chill of Washington, but the noise was stifling. Everywhere there were people shouting and yelling, but it was still not the city that he had once known. The taxi he had chosen looked brand new from the outside with a fresh paint job and no dents. It was a new hybrid model, the same as any cab he would have found in Washington. Nearly every car these days was a hybrid, but the newer models were not just electric and gas but also solar. The inside of the cab was clean. The only thing that gave him pause for thought was that the driver looked like a vagabond. He was unshaven, his hair a mess. He wore a yellow cab company uniform that looked pretty clean though, wrinkled but clean, so Jackson went ahead and hopped in.

He was struck by just how clean and orderly everything, other than his cab driver, looked. Mexico City had certainly come up in the world since joining the UCSA. Jackson was so engrossed in looking around him that it took him a moment to figure out that the cab wasn't moving, and he remembered that he hadn't given the driver an address.

"You go to Co-yo-Kan?" he pronounced carefully, aware of the fact that he might sound patronizing but not wanting to risk getting lost.

The driver looked at him puzzled for a moment, and then in clear English said: "Coyocan?"

"Um, yeah," said Jackson, suitably embarrassed. "What you said, I need to go there; here's the address."

He fumbled in his pocket for a second before producing a card and handing it to the driver. He looked at it, nodded, and handed it back before starting the engine and peeling away from the curb. He would stop at his hotel in Coyocan, have a shower and a shave that he probably desperately needed, and then go off to see the Vasquez family. He had their address, having gotten it from one of the clerks in the records office. Working for the government did have some advantages. It occurred to him once again how much easier this trip was for him that it would be for any normal citizen.

In all the time that he had been deployed in Mexico, which probably added up to several months over the years of his military life, he'd never really taken the time to learn the local language. Never really seen the point, if he was honest. He'd been a citizen of the then NAU, and since everybody wanted to court business with the NAU, everybody had learned English. That meant that it was easy to converse with just about anyone that wanted to make money off you. Now, of course, as part of the UCSA, Mexicans were required to speak English, though it was unlikely that all had learnt in such a short time. Jackson found himself wishing that he'd spent at least a few evenings learning how to say something more useful than "¿Dónde está el baño?" and "¿Cuántas?"

Well, actually, knowing where the bathroom is was pretty useful, he guessed, and could probably help him out. He did want to know how much people wanted him to pay for things. If he encountered someone who spoke only Spanish, then he was going to be in trouble.

He spent the rest of the trip watching the suburbs of Mexico City pass by, amazed at their cleanliness and at how seemingly prosperous the city now was. He was further amazed when the taxi drew up at his hotel, which he had been expecting to be an old, rundown motel. He shook his head as he looked out the window. He really needed to ditch some of the stereotypes he had about this country. He was pleasantly surprised at the fact that the hotel he'd randomly chosen looked way better than some of the fancier hotels that he'd stayed in while he was in the American section of the UCSA. He kept forgetting that Mexico was part of the UCSA now, and as such, could be expected to have much the same standards as well as the same laws and regulations. As long as he was here, he didn't need to worry because he was inside the UCSA and everything would be okay. The rest of the world might be going insane, but the UCSA was keeping things in order, and that now included Mexico.

Check in to the hotel was easy. Both receptionists spoke perfect English, and the process was no different than going down to check into one of the hotels in Chicago when they visited family. However, this hotel was a little different in that it was well decorated and pleasing to the eye. There were fresh flowers of almost every color of the rainbow elegantly arranged in the hallways, and the reception area and small restaurant smelled pleasantly of delicious pies, although he was pretty sure that they called them empañadas down here.

It was the first time he'd been in a hotel for a while, and the first time that he'd be sleeping without Courtney for longer than he could remember now. Idly, as he waited for the elevator, he wondered how he'd ever managed to spend so much time away from her when he was in the military. He missed her already, and he'd seen her just a few hours ago when she'd dropped him off at the airport. Mind you, he thought, as he stepped into the cool elevator and pressed the button for his floor, staying here was way better than being shipped off to a base God knows where.

He entered his room and stood in the middle of it, breathing in the quiet solitude. It was a spacious room with a large bed and wide windows looking out into the courtyard of the hotel. He wished he could stay here longer, relax and calm down a little bit, but he was in Mexico for a reason that he couldn't put it off. He needed to get himself ready, get out of here and make his way to Villa de Garcia, the address that he had for Vasquez's parents.

He went into the bathroom and turned on the shower, the cool water feeling good on his skin, especially after the hot and sweaty cab ride that he'd had. To be fair, the driver had mumbled something to him before he'd got in, but Jackson had thought it to be something about no smoking, which was ridiculous because no one smoked in cabs these days. But maybe it was a new UCSA rule for Mexico, he'd thought. It was only when they were already underway and Jackson had rolled up the windows and asked for the air to be switched on that he'd realized the mistake he'd made. There was no air conditioning, as the driver had informed him when he got in. He'd rolled the windows back down and dealt with the dust of the road and the tepid air coming in. Luckily, the ride hadn't been that long, at around thirty-five minutes or so.

After the hot, sticky seat of the cab and the dust of the road, Jackson was happy to have something cooling him down and cleaning him up. He stepped out of the shower and toweled himself dry, beads of water on his skin running over the swell of his muscles. All those mornings of exercising certainly paid off, and he found himself wondering if he could still run a Marine obstacle course. He might look into that when he got home, contact one of his old platoon mates to see if he could sneak onto one.

He walked over to the mirror and wiped off a little haze before examining his face. It might be only two o'clock in Mexico, but he definitely had a five o'clock shadow. He turned on the tap and let it warm a little as he got his shaving things from his toilet bag. It wasn't necessary, as he still looked presentable. If he'd been going to any other meeting, he might not have bothered, but this wasn't just any meeting. This was Vasquez's parents, and maybe even his young wife that he had made a widow. He wanted to look perfect.

He wanted to look as though he was definitely contrite, but he wasn't sure how to manage that. The best he could do was look presentable, and he tried as hard as he could. After shaving, he dressed in khakis and a light blue button down shirt with a starched collar. He looked in the mirror again: he decided that he looked like one of the cartel members that were so popular as the bad guys in action movies these days, and groaned.

He hoped that the way he was dressed wasn't going to offend the Vasquezes. He had other options—Courtney had packed what seemed like a hundred different outfits to choose from. He didn't have the strength to deal with going through them all; looking smart and clean was the best he could do. It was better, anyway, he thought, than showing up in a uniform. He looked himself up and down in the mirror and nodded, before giving himself a stern talking to.

"You are not gonna back out of this, Jackson," he said, grimly. "You are going to do this today."

He gave himself a long, hard stare, daring himself to give up now before he turned, grabbed his wallet and hotel keys and went back down to the hotel lobby. He walked intently, all his focus on the task ahead, and strode up to the concierge at her desk.

The girl looked up at him—her hair well done in a bun, her suit beautifully pressed and her eyes smiling—and in the most polite voice possible said, "Excuse me sir, what can I get for you?"

He kept his voice low, requesting, "Could you please get me a taxi, preferably one with air conditioning?"

She smiled and nodded, picking up the phone as she did so. "Of course, sir. A car should be waiting for you at the door as soon as you walk out. Is a town car appropriate? I think you'll find it more comfortable than a taxi."

She was looking at his clean clothes as she said this, and Jackson thought that he must have cleaned up well to get this offer so he nodded. A town car would probably be considerably more expensive than a cab, but for the added price, at least the air conditioning would work, and hopefully the driver would smell a whole lot better than his last one. He smiled at the concierge who was already speaking on the phone, and walked towards the revolving door.

Sure enough, the car was just pulling up as he exited. Maybe they had cars on call, he thought. Before he got in, he made sure to ask about the air conditioning, and the driver, neat in a full uniform, looked at him like he was crazy before assuring him that the car was cooled with a functioning system.

Jackson slid into the long, leather seat and sighed in pleasure. It was a beautiful car, and he was determined to take one like it to the airport the next day. He sat back and did his best to relax as the car conveyed him to the Vasquezes home.

Villa de Garcia, Mexico, UCSA

The driver announced that they would arrive at the Villa de Garcia around an hour later, and Jackson silently thanked the receptionist for getting him the town car instead of a cab. The city was well into rush hour now, and the ride had taken far longer than he'd expected, but he'd been safe inside his cool, luxurious cocoon. As the car pulled up to a house, he looked out the window and saw an opulent villa, not at all what he had been expecting. He'd been under the impression that he was going to the home of a poorer family, but this place was lavish. After all the times that Vasquez has told him about sending money to his mother, father, and pregnant wife, and after meeting the Vasquez's once before, he had been certain that they lived in a meager home, maybe even in an apartment.

The car drew up in front of the white mission style house, surrounded by some of the greenest grass that Jackson had ever seen. It was an older home, to be sure, but it was well taken care of and maintained. It was definitely the home of someone with some amount of money. Surely there was some kind of mistake here? But the driver examined the address that Jackson had been given and shook his head. No, this was the place.

Jackson got out of the car and walked the neatly kept gravel path to the large, double front door. He took a deep breath in and out, finger hovering over the doorbell, but he just couldn't do it. He needed to try again. Turning around, he walked back to the town car, where the driver stared at him.

"If you wait here until I get back, I'll pay you for another fare," he said, leaning in to speak through the half open driver's side window.

The driver looked hesitant. "Not necessary, sir. This ride and the ride back are courtesy of the hotel. But please hurry. This place gets dangerous at night. The cartels are very powerful around here."

Weird, thought Jackson. How could that be? Everything he'd read had said that the cartels were on their way out. Maybe the driver just didn't follow the news. Or maybe, he thought, he was just angling for more money. Well, today was his lucky day, since Jackson didn't feel like being stranded here if the door was slammed in his face.

"In that case, I'll tip you very well for staying as long as I need you to. Okay?" he asked, briskly.

The driver nodded his head and slid the car into park. He turned off the engine, but left the car on, reaching down to switch on the radio as Jackson turned and once again walked his way up the gravel path. As he walked, he heard the sounds of a soccer game and heard the driver's voice shouting, "Goal!"

Again he faced the big double doors, and again he breathed in deeply and then out again, calming his mind and achieving some kind of focus. He held his finger just above the doorbell and steeled himself. He had to do what he had to do, and had paid good money and spent a fair amount of time, not to mention a few favors, getting all the way down here for this moment. He needed to confront these people, to apologize, to try get rid of these damn nightmares. Yet still he didn't press the doorbell. After five, he decided, and began to count in his head. Before he got to five, the door opened.

"Hello," said a young girl, no more than thirteen or so, looking at him curiously.

Jackson was dumbstruck and stood there looking at her while she began to worry about this strange man on the doorstep.

"Can I help you?" she prompted, looking like she was about to slam the door in his face.

"Um, um, yes," he said, regaining his tongue. "Um, hi. I'm looking for Mr. and Mrs. Vasquez." He was still pretty certain that he was at the wrong house.

"Let me get my mom," said the girl, her English perfect as she looked at him suspiciously and then swung the door closed.

He was still thinking that he might run away as he waited on the small porch. He could run over to the car, slide into the back seat, and they'd peel off as if they were being chased by a group of movie-style henchmen. But he was rooted to the spot. He'd forgotten to tell the driver to keep the engine running anyhow, so it probably wouldn't work like it did in the movies. He just stood, feeling like an idiot, as he waited for someone to come back. Finally, the door did open again, this time revealing the girl and Mrs. Vasquez.

"Hola," said the woman, looking at Jackson. "I'm Mrs. Vasquez. Can I help you?"

She was dressed in a flowing blue dress and obviously didn't recognize him. Well, that was alright, he thought. He certainly looked different out of uniform, and they really had only met in passing as Vasquez was showing his parents around the base.

"Yes," he said, uncertainly. "I, um, knew your son, Armani. I wanted to know if I could talk with you and your husband."

A cloud passed over the woman's face at the pain of the name of her dead son, but she still managed to speak. "You knew mi hijo?" she asked.

"Who?" asked Jackson, confused.

"It means 'my son' in Spanish," said the girl, helpfully.

Mrs. Vasquez had far more of an accent than her daughter did. "Oh," said Jackson. "Yes, yes, I knew him."

"Come on in," Mrs. Vasquez said, holding the door open wider. Then she turned to the young girl. "Make sure that you come back before dark."

The girl nodded and skipped off down the path.

"I didn't know that Armani had a sister," he commented as he watched her go.

"Ah, yes," said Mrs. Vasquez, smiling at her daughter. "He also had a wife and a lovely baby girl. But I'm sure you knew that already, no? His wife moved out of this house and back with her parents. That's where my daughter was going, to see her niece."

She was obviously making small talk, and Jackson nodded. "Yes, of course," he said. "Vasquez spoke often of his girl."

They were standing in the middle of a large open hall, a curving staircase rising up to a balcony above them, and Mrs. Vasquez gestured at him to follow her. "Come, my husband is in the living room. Oh, it's always so nice to meet Armani's friends."

Jackson wondered how long that attitude was going to last, but he followed her as she walked towards an open door.

"Roberto," she spoke loudly. "Roberto, it's one of Armani's friends come to see us."

They entered the living room and Jackson saw a rotund, older man sitting in a chair. Looking closely he could just make out the outlines of Armani's high cheekbones in the older man's face. The man struggled up out of his chair, smoothing his hair to make himself look more presentable, stumbling as he did so. Then he held out a hand that Jackson took and shook. Obviously Vasquez's father recognized him no more than his mother did, but that was hardly surprising as the man was obviously drunk.

"Hello," said Jackson. It was time, and there was no use beating around the bush. He needed to state his business before these people offered him any kind of hospitality. "My name is Anthony Jackson. We've actually met before at the army base, but only briefly. I was friends with Armani, and I've come here to ask your forgiveness."

Mrs. Vasquez's eyes widened slightly as her husband said, "Forgiveness?" He slurred the word a little. "Forgiveness for what?"

Jackson took a deep breath. "I was the one that killed your son," he said loudly and clearly so that there could be no mistake. He didn't think that he could say it again.

"¡Dios mío! ¿Por qué vienes aquí, cabrón?"

Roberto Vasquez pulled back his arm and prepared to take a swing at Jackson. Even though Jackson spoke only a handful of words of Spanish, he knew enough to know that Vasquez's father was calling him a bastard and asking what the hell he was doing here.

Mrs. Vasquez pulled back on her husband's arm, her face sad, but her voice firm. "Roberto, calm down please. You know what the doctor said."

Stunned by her calm and grace, Jackson could feel tears pricking at his eyes. He had no idea how he would react if Roberto Vasquez was admitting to killing one of his daughters.

"I just wanted to say sorry, though I know it doesn't help. I felt you deserved my apology face to face. I shot only because Armani was reloading his weapon. I tried to stop him from doing it. I didn't mean to..." He wiped his eyes and trailed off.

Señora Vasquez was still holding on to her husband's arm, and Jackson saw pain on her face, an awful kind of acceptance as she said, "Thank you for coming to apologize, Anthony, but I think that maybe you should go."

Jackson nodded. Mr. Vasquez moved a step closer to him but seemed less set on violence. He smelled like the inside of a bar.

"It's not your fault," he said in a voice heavy with defeat. "It's not your fault." Tears were falling from his eyes, rolling down rugged, wrinkled cheeks. "Está zorra le vendió como una idiota. Todo era para ese malvado en la capital."

Mr. Vasquez's English had deserted him, and while Jackson could make out the words, he didn't understand what was being said. Regardless, it was clearly time to leave. He bade both farewell and made his own way to the door, wondering what Mr. Vasquez had said, but deciding it was of little importance. He'd done what he needed to do, done all he could so he left the house and went back to the car, telling the driver to take him back to the hotel.

As the car pulled away, he found himself looking at the house and wondering. He didn't have the feeling that this had been a family house, didn't feel that children had grown up in it. Roberto Vasquez particularly hadn't seemed especially at ease in such a place. He wondered again where the money for the house had come from. Maybe some kind of insurance, he figured, and put the issue to rest.

That night he slept soundly, knowing that this hadn't been his fault. He'd needed to hear that from someone connected to and hurt by the incident. Courtney had been right: this had been the right thing to do.

11

THE FOURTH YEAR

June 18th, 2079
Alexandria, Virginia, UCSA
Article Originally Published in *UCSA Today*, Reused with Permission
Annual UCSA Day Protest Smaller Than Usual
Jake Kelly, Stringer

Protesters were present as usual in our great nation's capital as we celebrated the annual federal holiday of UCSA Day, the day when we remember those that passed during the great attacks of 2051 and celebrate the founding of our country. While processions, speeches and fireworks were the order of the day, there were still several dissenters who saw fit to mar such a great occasion with their presence.

Fortunately, it appears as though President Meyers's stringent defense policies are paying off, as the number of protesters was distinctly down over previous years. While it is usual that the number of protesters falls year on year, a mark no doubt of the growing confidence of people in the nation's leadership, this year we were fortunate enough to see a drop of almost fifty percent in the number of those seen protesting UCSA Day. Clearly, stringent measures work best with such people, and in order to see a further stunning fall in next year's processes, the government should see fit to increase punitive measures for those found to be espousing dissident or even Apocalytic ideals.

Such a day of great joy can only be a reminder of how truly prosperous and successful our country is. Let us all hope that next year we can enjoy such an occasion without the presence of misled, mentally unstable, or downright misinformed protesters.

■ ■ ■

Jackson ignored the article as he was too busy thinking to want to read it. Instead, he looked out of the big picture window in the living room at the home down the street. It had once belonged to a family called the Walkers, a pleasant family with two kids just a little older than his own. While they were not close friends, they had run into one another at school and neighborhood social events. Now the house was being roped off and boarded up by federal agents. No one was to enter the home until the investigation was finished, which could be a long time from now. He was seeing this happen more and more lately, seeing boarded-up houses on his way to work, and even knew some of the people who had once occupied them. Every now and again, you'd go to sleep thinking that your next door neighbor was a straight, stand-up guy, and then you'd wake up the next morning and find that he'd been an operative for Hariq Jihad. He'd be gone and his family with him.

There had been so many Hariq Jihad operatives found in the years since Espinoza's assassination that it was scary if you thought about it too much. It was as if a sudden chasm opened up and out flowed thousands of dissidents and enemies of the state. Though it was, he supposed, simply an illusion. Probably it was just that the new laws and rules made it easier to find such people who had always existed rather than that there were more of them around. There was always, if he was honest with himself, the fear that one day they'd come for you—that you might make a mistake and it would be your house that was boarded up. There had been so many new rules enacted since the Second Alien and Sedition Act had passed that sometimes it seemed impossible to keep up with them all. Maybe he, or someone he knew, could break one of these rules without even knowing it existed.

Jackson had never really bothered to stay on top of politics all that much, despite working in the White House. He read the articles and certainly overheard things while working. He wasn't a politician and wasn't that interested in it. He was a soldier at heart, the go-to guy for President Meyer since he'd been picked for the president's personal security detail, but that was all. He wasn't someone who could effectively analyze or judge the actions of the government. He knew the president, and knew he was a good and decent man who wouldn't do wrong. He protected his country. Still, it was worrisome, he thought, as he watched an agent seal up another window across the street. Who doesn't worry when people go missing in the middle of the night?

He didn't know what to say when his kids asked, which was the real problem for him. It was tough to explain things like this to them, especially now that they were growing older and were naturally curious about the world around them. Maya was a particular worry, and he distinctly remembered a conversation they'd had a week or so ago.

"Whatever happened to the Jamisons?" Maya had asked.

She had played with Mac and Tammy Jamison's son, Rick, in the past, although they'd never exactly been best friends. They were at the age when there was a clear difference between boys and girls, so they weren't that close.

With a sigh, he thought about what to tell her. He worried about Maya and some of her proclivities. She was so in love with the past, history and the concept of liberty. Ideals that weren't necessarily bad ones, or even dangerous ones if channeled in the right way, but still worrying ones because it was a thin line. She could, for example, make an excellent teacher of UCSA history, produce excellent propaganda, or even become an academic at a university, but only so long as she remembered the difference between the past and now.

Sometimes he'd think about her while he was busy trying to protect the president and worry about her future. He worried that she wasn't really meant for this world at all. He dared to hope that he had taught her enough about life and being loyal to her country that she wouldn't get involved with either the Hariq Jihad or the Apocalytes. Then he'd shake his head and tell himself not to be so stupid. Maya was a good smart kid and she'd never fall for anything like that. Her interest was a natural and academic one, not one that she would seriously consider believing in. He had raised a good kid, one who knew how to think and was a responsible and loyal member of society, not some rebel. He had nothing to worry about.

So he had answered her question honestly. "They were caught as members of the Hariq Jihad," he'd told her. He wished that would be the end of the matter, because he really didn't want to discuss it.

Maya looked thoughtful, putting down the book she had been reading. "You know," she said, "Janie at school told me that her uncle Peter went missing. Do you think he was a member of one of those groups?"

Jackson shrugged. "It's possible, sweetie. You never know nowadays."

His daughter pouted a little as she always did when thinking, and he had to bite back a smile at how he could still see his little girl in what was now the beautiful face of a young woman.

"But," she said, "don't we have, like, the right to a fair trial and stuff? They can't just take people in the night, can they?"

"It isn't like that," he said, trying to remain patient with her. "This is a different issue. Of course we do, but terrorists don't, and we have to protect ourselves from terrorists." His voice started to rise a little because he was getting annoyed with the conversation, irritated with his daughter for starting it and annoyed with himself for being upset because she was asking reasonable questions but ones that made him uncomfortable. Deep down, the same questions bothered him, too.

"It's just," and she paused for a second, as though trying to think of the right words. "It's just that I think I read somewhere that Ben Franklin said that if you give up necessary liberty for temporary security, you lose both."

It took Jackson a second to process this, and then he asked, confused, "Ben who?"

"Franklin," Maya explained. "He was one of the people that founded the old United States of America."

"You need to stop," he managed to spit out through clenched teeth.

In one stride, he was next to the couch and grabbing her arm, giving her a jolt to let her know just how serious what she had just said was. "You need to stop talking like this right now."

He took a breath, trying to calm himself down, trying not to lose his temper anymore than he already had. She wasn't involved in anything, he told himself. She was just a foolish girl that read too much, that was all, but she had to understand that things like this could get her labeled as a terrorist—could get them all labeled as terrorists. He knew that she wasn't, of course, and she definitely wasn't one of those religious Apocalyte nuts, but other people didn't know her as well as he did. Other people could make mistakes. She was a good girl, she believed in the UCSA and all that it stood for. She wouldn't go along with the type of people that believed in fringe stuff. This was some kind of phase. It was going to be okay.

"I'm sorry," she said, her face going red as tears formed in her eyes.

Barely able to look him in the eye, she shook off his hand and ran out of the room. Jackson tried to think of something to say but then heard the loud bang of Maya's bedroom door slamming. The steady thud of her music began as she switched on the radio. He knew it was no use talking to her now, as it would take a few hours for her to calm down and be willing to listen to anything he had to say. She was always like that. It took a fair amount to make her lose it—she wasn't as moody as most teenagers he'd heard about—but it took time for her to calm herself as well. He might as well leave it for now.

He sank down onto the couch, the cushion still warm where Maya had been sitting, and sighed. He regretted ever getting her any of those books and trinkets that she'd pleaded for. He was sure that it was all his fault that she was talking like this—not that there was anything seriously wrong, as this was just a phase. He'd thought she'd understood how dangerous this all was—how dangerous it could be to speak the way she had spoken. All he wanted was for her to go back to being his little girl. The little girl that he'd loved and cared for all those years ago, not this new creature that had opinions different from his own. But if he were truthful, he knew that he'd barely known Maya as a little girl and had gone months without even seeing her when he was deployed. He was proud that his daughter was a strong enough woman to have her own opinions; they just couldn't be these opinions, that's all.

People had disappeared, he knew that, and he'd heard talk of it in the capitol. He knew that people were scared; even he was a little scared, just in case, because you never knew. No one wanted to discuss the disappearances because they were afraid that, if they did, then they too would be found on the list, that list of people who would disappear. It was hysteria, he thought, paranoia, but at the same time he found himself breathing a little harder, his heart racing a little, whenever he thought about the disappeared people. He was glad no one could read his thoughts.

At some point, many of the disappeared would resurface. They had been rehabilitated, reminded of what a great country the UCSA was. They wouldn't be upset about things anymore, and they'd go back to being well-liked citizens. They would start new jobs and be productive members of society again for a while. Somehow this rehabilitation never seemed to last, though, as people would go back to their old habits. If and when they did, they'd be arrested again and charged with sedition.

In these cases, the lucky ones were given a trial, though those highly suspected or caught in the act of something were not tried at all. If given a trial, the accused faced the death penalty, but the smart ones repented their crimes against the state and instead served years in prison on indeterminate sentences to be released only when the authorities were assured of their rehabilitation again. Even those not given a trial were given chance after chance to repent their crimes, often in public or on television. Yet in many cases, it was already too late for mercy to be applied to their crimes and they would be executed.

Other than sedition, terrorism was the other big crime, and in these cases there were no trials. Suspects were taken to detention centers: large, crowded buildings much like the high security jails of old. They were often violent and uncomfortable. There, suspects would wait for a judicial review of their record, something that could take months or even years, with detention centers packed full with the backlog of potential criminals. Hopefully nothing would be found in this review, but all too often something was. The national review service had been highly efficient in making sure that only people with real problems were arrested—real terrorists. It might be hard to believe that some of the pimply faced teenagers paraded on television were terrorists, but the Hariq Jihad got to them early. They would recruit in schools where children were impressionable. It was tough for agents to identify the recruiters though, and often it was unclear who gave the orders and ran the operation. The agencies always erred on the side of caution and arrested the suspect anyway.

Finding men and women who worked directly with the Hariq Jihad was tough, but finding Apocalytes was far easier. Apocalytes were difficult to figure out. Jackson had never really understood how they lived such old-fashioned lives and how they could believe in such old-fashioned principles, let alone how they could honestly think that there was a God that wished to destroy such a socially progressive state as the UCSA. They were relatively easy to find, though. They were paraded on television, their old-fashioned clothes marking them as true Apocalytes. They were less to be worried about, but Apocalytes were still enemies of the state, and therefore had to be punished. Members were often considered insane since they refused public tribunals. Their crimes were confessed in private, but no one was interested in their insane ramblings.

This was what Jackson was worried about. He was worried that Maya could be following these same paths. He didn't want to have to find a way to smooth things over with the government so that his daughter could get special treatment. He didn't want to pull in favors because she made a stupid mistake and hadn't learned well enough to keep quiet. What if something like this did happen? Well, he would save her, he thought. It would be his duty, not just as her father, but also because he had nurtured this fascination with the past.

He shook his head slowly. Having kids was never supposed to be easy, he guessed, but both his daughters had been easy toddlers. They'd never been in trouble, had good grades, and were polite and beautiful too. He supposed that it was only fair that he experience some of the pains of being a parent to a teenager. Maya would grow out of this, he was sure. But in the meantime, he was going to have to keep an eye on her.

Courtney came in to the living room, her head half-buried in a magazine. He smiled, glad that she'd gone back to work, if only part-time. It gave her outside interests and didn't appear to affect the way the house was run in the slightest.

"Hi honey," he said.

"Hi there."

She bent over and kissed him, noticing the book beside him and frowning. Then she looked up at the ceiling where loud music was thumping away in Maya's bedroom, putting two and two together.

"Aha," she said. "So what's wrong with Maya then?"

Jackson played dumb, shrugged, and said: "She's a teenager, honey. We knew this time would come. She's just sulking. I'll go up and talk to her later."

Courtney shook her head. "It had to happen sometime," she said. "Just when I was starting to think that we'd escaped this whole teenage thing with Maya."

"It'll pass," Jackson said, holding out his arms so that his wife could perch on his lap. "It'll pass."

It would pass, and Courtney wasn't going to hear about any of this crap. No point in the both of them being worried, after all. He looked over her shoulder to the window where he could see the Walker's house, now firmly boarded up. They weren't going to be the next disappearing family, he vowed.

■ ■ ■

April, earlier that year

The Jamisons were a nice family of four that lived just next door in a fake Tudor style house that always looked well-kept. Tammy and Mac came over from time to time for dinner, and the kids played together due more to proximity than common interests. Sometimes they grilled together in their back yards.

Mac had fallen on hard times recently and was working part-time in a manufacturing plant in the area. It wasn't fun work, he'd said, but it was honest work for the benefit of the United Continental States of America, and he was proud to do it. Later, Jackson would distinctly remember him saying this, remember the look on his face as he said it, the real, honest pride that shone there. That was one of the things that confused him. He knew that Mac was a good guy, but a guy that was having a tough time in the world right now, what with his job problems and all. Things would get better for Mac, though, he was sure. Things were prosperous for the nation as a whole, and it was definitely better here than in Europe or elsewhere in the world. No matter what else happened, things were getting better and they'd get better for the Jamisons too, Jackson knew it.

Tammy Jamison was pretty and smart as well as being a great cook. Sometimes she and Courtney shared recipes, and Jackson admitted only to himself that Tammy's brownies were some of the best he'd ever tasted in his life. She'd been a teacher, he'd learned from Courtney, at a local parochial school. However, with the changes in the country those kind of schools simply weren't required anymore, so she took a new job as an assistant teacher at the local elementary school. She left for work with a smile every day, but Jackson thought that deep down she must have hated it. He knew that she'd been one of the best teachers at the Holy Cross Lutheran School. She'd had her own classroom and made her own lesson plans. She could spend as much time as she wanted on any subject she chose. One night after one glass of wine too many, Tammy had shared her irritation with her current job and had spoken of her previous role as the best job. Since the government had gotten so involved in the curriculum, there was no deviation from the set of books, lectures, and materials taught in the classroom from kindergarten to doctorate programs.

He was all too familiar with this himself, since his two daughters were in school during these years of change. He'd had to help both MacKenzie and Maya deal with these dramatic changes in the educational system, though it was Maya who had the most problems. Maya was the more creative of the sisters, and she wanted to have long talks about concepts and ideas. The new curriculum didn't allow for learners like Maya. The content was heavy in patriotism and grew commitment to the United Continental

States of America to foster citizenship that would strengthen the nation. The country needed citizens that could build the future and ensure the success of the nation. Not that Jackson thought his daughter was not any of these things; she very much was, but not in the way her teachers preferred. It was because of this that he allowed her to carve her own path at home, often indulging her with books and discussions—the things that she thirsted for but didn't get at school.

The Jamison kids, Rick and Grace, were wonderfully well behaved. Thinking back, Jackson couldn't remember a single situation where either Rick or Grace had gotten into trouble. His kids were well behaved too, but Rick and Grace were something else— like perfect little angels. He wouldn't have traded his family for the world, even if Maya did sometimes sulk and MacKenzie could whine from time to time. Better that than the occasionally scary perfection of Rick and Grace; he joked they were like programmed robots at times.

He watched one afternoon as Mac came home, dirty and exhausted looking, his face and hands grimy. Jackson was out in the yard watching the kids play and Mac came around the side of the house, a cold beer in his dirty hands, his face looking drawn. Jackson knew that he worked in one of the weapons manufacturing plants, and that it must be tough work. No one really knew why the UCSA had any need to amass huge stockpiles of weaponry. It wasn't like they were involved in any of the various wars going on around the world these days. Hariq Jihad seemed to be fading into the recent past, having not perpetrated a successful attack in years. The government motto was "better vigilant than victim," and Jackson believed that. He, for one, wanted to make sure that his country was strong and ready if any terrorist tried to pull off a wicked plan. Plus, he thought, keeping the weapons manufacturing plants opened meant that there were plenty of jobs around for people like Mac, so that was a bonus, too.

Jackson paused, looking at the girls playing, drinking the site in. This is what he'd dreamed of in his last military tour—this was the kind of father he'd always wanted to be. He was in his very own back yard, home from work early for the second time this week, able to watch his kids and smile with them.

"Where do they get all that energy from?"

Mac had spotted him and came to the fence that separated their two yards, an extra beer in his hand that he popped open and passed over to Jackson, who thanked him.

"No idea," said Jackson, watching the kids start to tear around the swing set at the bottom of the garden. "Wish I could get some of it for myself though."

"Tell me about it," said Mac, grinning at the kids but his eyes looking far away.

"You must be bushed," Jackson said. "Really takes it out of you going down to that plant, doesn't it?"

Mac nodded. "Sure does."

Jackson thought for a few minutes. "Why don't you look for something else, Mac?" he asked. "I could put in a good word for you if you think it'd help. I mean, I know it's been a bit tough for you of late, but there's plenty of work going around now, you know that. I'm sure you could find something a bit less back-breaking."

Almost immediately, Jackson sensed that he'd said the wrong thing as Mac's face got a little stonier and he shook his head.

"Happy where I am, thanks, Jackson," he said.

"I'm sorry," said Jackson. "I overstepped the line there. My bad. That was out of order."

Mac smiled again, letting a deep breath go. "Nah, you're alright Jackson. I see how it must look to you, but I'm actually happy. I'm doing something important. I'm helping the country, and that's the way I want it to be. You're probably right that I could find something better, but fact is that I just don't want to, not right yet. I like sweating it out, knowing that I'm doing something directly helpful, you know? I feel like I'm really helping build this country, that I'm really playing my part, and I like that."

"What did you do before?" Jackson asked, curiously, leaning his elbow on the fence and taking a sip from his beer.

"Advertising," sniffed Mac. "Hated it. All that lying and manipulating wasn't for me. That's um, well, that's kinda how I ended up here like this."

"What do you mean?"

Mac chuckled. "Lost it with a client. He asked me to promise one thing in an ad but to put so many restrictions in the small print at the bottom that no one could possibly qualify. I about punched him. My boss thought it best if I took a permanent vacation."

Jackson laughed at this. "You serious?"

"Serious as a heart attack," said Mac. "And there's no way I'm going back to something like that."

They watched as the kids reversed direction and began running the other way. Mac became pensive.

"We're doing it for them," he said, after a while. "Building them a new country, a safe one. There's nothing I wouldn't do for my kids. I want them to be able to think of me when I'm gone and think that I did my part. You were a Marine, Jackson, you did your part. You saved the president's life; I've heard all about it. So maybe this sounds dumb to you, but working, going out there every day and working my ass off, that's me doing my part, helping make this country great. Helping my kids be safe and wishing them a future."

"It doesn't sound dumb at all," said Jackson. "Makes perfect sense." And it did.

It was two days later that Courtney shook him awake.

"They're gone," she said, urgently. "Gone."

"Who? What?" he asked, groggily.

"I got up early, went down to switch the coffee on, and you know how you can see through the kitchen window across into the yard of the Jamisons and to where they got that new sliding door fitted and..."

"You're rambling," Jackson said, sitting up in bed. "Try and focus, hun. It's early and I don't have much brain."

Courtney swallowed. "And the Jamisons are gone. Disappeared. The house is boarded up."

Jackson shook his head. "No, no," he said. "They've probably just gone on vacation or something." But he knew even as he said it that they hadn't. They wouldn't have gone without saying something, passing along a spare key to get the plants watered. The family definitely wouldn't have gone during school time.

He did his best to find out what had happened, pulling strings and talking to people around the White House, listening in on the gossip. He was able to piece together that the Jamisons had been picked up during the night, just like everyone else was. As for a reason? Mac was using his position in the manufacturing plant to pass along plans and materials to Hariq Jihad. Was that why he'd been so stubborn about not changing his job? Because he was working as an operative? Jackson considered this for a long while but just couldn't accept it, couldn't reconcile the man he had known with the crimes he was accused of.

The worst was what the future held for them. Both Tammy and Mac had been under surveillance due to their past occupations, and now Mac was being charged with terrorist acts rather than sedition, so there was to be no trial. This stunned Jackson, and he didn't know what to do with the information. Surely he could have a word with someone? Maybe write some kind of recommendation letter? He didn't believe for a second that the Jamisons were anything other than loyal citizens and he'd lived next door to them for a few years. He decided to take a day or so to make a firm decision, as he didn't want to rush things and maybe destroy his only chance of helping his neighbors.

An hour later, as he was about to leave his post outside the president's door, the front door to the oval office as always, Mitzy got a phone call then looked at him.

"Hey, Jackson," she said. "The president asked if you can pop inside his office for a minute before you go off duty."

He frowned. That was pretty unusual. Sure, he had meetings with the president about security matters, but they were usually planned well in advance to accommodate the president's busy schedule. Still, maybe something had come up. He straightened his tie a little and Mitzy winked at him.

"You look stunning," she said, obviously trying to soothe his nerves.

Opening the door, he went in to the office where Meyers was sitting behind his desk.

"Take a seat, Jackson," the president said, giving his famous smile. "Just wanted a word is all."

Doing as he was told, he sat at the other side of the desk, the window behind the president looking out over the famous rose garden, and waited.

"Listen, Jackson, it's come to my attention that you've been asking some questions—something about a guy called Jamison, a friend of yours maybe?"

Jackson frowned again. "Yes, but, um..."

Meyers waved a hand. "I thought I told you when I offered you this job that I know everything," he said, teasing. "How I know doesn't matter, but the fact that I know does, because that means other people know and have taken note. You're my top security guy; I don't want to lose you, and I certainly don't want the embarrassment of your name being connected to that of a terrorist. So I'm telling you now, as a friend as well as your leader, that you need to be careful."

Nodding, Jackson said, "Of course, sir. I'm sorry for any embarrassment I've caused."

"No more questions," said Meyers. "And, if I might say so, a little more faith in the system might be expected from you."

Suddenly aware of the very dangerous thing he'd been doing, not to mention what he'd been about to do by writing a letter of recommendation, Jackson felt sick to his stomach.

"Of course, sir," he said. "I have never had anything but complete faith in and loyalty to our country."

"I know that, Jackson," Meyers said, evenly. "That's why you're here and I'm telling you this. I know it's your loyalty to this nation and its people that has brought about this conversation. You're loyal to your friend and you want to help. While I admire you for that, it's not a good idea with what we have to deal with day in and day out. Now I'm going to do you a huge favor and forget that we even had this conversation. It will never be referred to again. Understood?"

"Sir, yes sir," said Jackson, standing up as he was obviously being dismissed.

He made it out of the office and across the hall into the nearest bathroom before he vomited up his breakfast, getting spots on his tie. Then, legs still shaking, he leaned against the cold tiles of the wall and cursed himself. How could he have been such an idiot? How? Never again, he vowed. Never again would he show to anyone that he was anything less than a perfect and loyal citizen.

■ ■ ■

The night after the argument with Maya, Jackson couldn't sleep. He hadn't had the chance to speak to his daughter again before she'd switched out her light and feigned sleep. Courtney had turned in early, and Jackson was left sitting and reading in the living room, hoping to tire himself out before he went up to bed. His mind kept circling back to the Walkers, the Jamisons, and the pleasant, unremarkable, nice people with the new baby next door. He could see Mac's face, but he was terrified, trying to shelter his wife and kids from the violence of the detention center. There had been no news of what became of the family. He wondered if he should reach out to old friends to make sure they hadn't disappeared. Had the woman with the screaming toddler at the grocery store made it home or was she taken before she could make it home to start dinner? Maya's words cast a shadow over his thoughts like a dark cloud. His stomach felt twisted in knots, not unlike the feeling he had the morning the president told him to stop asking questions.

He sighed and put his own book down, looking around the living room lit by pools of light from lamps. Finally, he saw what he was looking for. Courtney must have put Maya's book out of the way on the side table. He got up and grabbed the book, scanning for Maya's highlights until he found what he was looking for.

"If you give up necessary liberty for temporary security, you lose both."

He ran his finger under the words. The line was followed by a long explanation of all the fallacies of the quote; this was no seditious book. In fact, turning it over, Jackson saw that it was a university history text—something that Maya really wasn't old enough to be reading and yet one that he'd probably bought for her without realizing.

He took the book back to his chair and read the line again and again. Was that what was happening here? He couldn't fault the government for keeping them safe from terrorist attacks, and certainly laws and regulations were necessary to keep things safe. But were things starting to go too far?

Jackson groaned and closed the book. How the hell was he supposed to answer a question like that? He knew nothing about politics. He was a soldier, but the disappeared people bothered him. The memory of the Jamisons bothered him. He was beginning to wish that he hadn't heard any of this. He wanted to be a regular guy and bury his head in the sand. If he had been more skeptical from the beginning and less of a follower, would anything be different now? Governments make mistakes, he reminded himself. The Jamisons were obviously mistakes. But did all the thousands of successful terrorist mistakes make up for that one mistake? Logically, he knew that they did. Yet in his heart, he couldn't bring himself to believe it.

Another quote that he had heard long ago in reference to the Nazis popped into his head: "The end justifies the means." He couldn't place it but knew that it was something to do with the justification for genocide. He wasn't sure that was the case here and decided all he could do was hope that he and his family never joined that list of mistakes.

12

THE FIFTH YEAR

May 30th, 2080

May 30th, 2080
Meyers Confederacy High School, Alexandria, Virginia, UCSA
Article Originally Published in the *Maryland Sentinel*, Reused with Permission

Dissenters Disrupt Memorial Day Festivities
Mark H. Finnegan, Crime Editor

Memorial Day is traditionally a somber occasion to remember those who have been lost defending our country while celebrating those who still serve in protecting us all. It is also a day when we remember the passing of the great National Defense Act that protects our great nation. And yet, on this most solemn of occasions, dissidents still feel it necessary to make their presence felt.

Most citizens agree that the passage of the National Defense Act has been a boon to us all. The Act, passed four years ago, gave unlimited powers to the UCSA Department of Defense to ensure the protection of our great nation against the threat of Hariq Jihad and any other terrorist organizations that wished the UCSA harm. Passed in response to the assassination of then-President of Mexico Espinoza and the attempted assassination of our own President Meyers, the Act was assurance to us all that our nation would not run in the face of terrorist threats.

Billions upon billions of dollars have been rightfully poured into the protection of our country, and the Act has been hailed as an astounding success. Not one single successful plot has come to fruition in the UCSA since the Act was passed. Partially, of course, this is due to the fact that agencies now have the power to seek out, find and incarcerate terrorists before actions are carried out, as opposed to in the past where enough evidence to prove guilt had to be found to hold a trial. The abandonment of the trial process for those accused of terrorism has done so much, not just to save the country money, but also to speed up and ease the process by which terrorists can be isolated from law-abiding citizens.

The Act also pushed into effect serious restrictions on travel, further reinforcing more lenient measures in the Alien and Sedition Act II, and making it far easier for authorities to track and block terrorist movement within the country.

However, despite more and more laws coming into effect to try to curb the activities of terrorists and dissenters alike, once more we were greeted with the disgusting sight of protesters at this year's Memorial Day celebrations. How long, we wonder, must decent citizens be forced to watch such actions, to listen to such heresies? How long before such disrespect will be squashed like the proverbial bug that it is?

Police action was immediate and, through the use of both chemical weapons such as smoke bombs and pepper spray as well as the use of more traditional weapons, the protest was quickly dispersed. Perhaps it is time, however, for prevention rather than cure?

President Meyers has expressed his profound sadness and disgust at the events of the Memorial Day celebration, and has promised that action will be taken to prevent future displays of such atrocity. An announcement is expected later this week concerning new proposed laws that would keep dissenters off the streets and away from government sanctioned celebrations such as Memorial Day. Readers can only hope that these measures will be stringent enough to preserve the sanctity of next year's celebrations.

■ ■ ■

Jackson read the news clipping that was pinned to the wall in the school foyer as part of a display on how the government successfully protected the nation. In the very center of the display was a large smiling portrait of Meyers, one that Jackson had seen several times before.

The building smelled like any other school he'd ever been in—a mixture of teenage hormones, cafeteria food and industrial cleaning products—reminding him of his own school days. Not that Meyers Middle School was anything like the school he'd attended in Chicago. No, this was a clean, well-maintained building with body scanners and security checks at every door, smiling portraits of the president in every room, and an efficient air conditioning system.

It wasn't the first time he'd been here. He'd attended parent–teacher conferences, and had even given a speech at career day extolling the virtues of joining the Protection Forces that he hoped had inspired at least some kids to sign up. Today would probably be the last time he was here. Maya was about to graduate, so he looked around with a certain amount of nostalgia.

He couldn't help but remember Maya's sixth grade graduation, when he'd just gotten home from the military, unsure whether his marriage was going to work out. Now, here they were, five years later, and all was great. Actually, they were better than great; they were perfect. Maya had skipped a grade in high school, hardly surprising given her natural intelligence and the new federal schooling system had eliminated the fourth year of high school. There were fewer subjects, with the removal of foreign languages and many of the art classes. Schools also focused far less on subjects such as history. That meant that his little girl was sweet sixteen and about to become a graduate, and he couldn't be prouder.

"Come on, Ant," Courtney said, coming back to the foyer and finding him staring at the wall. "We're about to get started in there and don't want to be late. MacKenzie's holding our place in line."

With a sigh, Jackson followed his wife to stand in the long line of parents and relatives waiting outside of the auditorium. There was no more chaos and rushing to get a good seat on the bleachers. Everything here was formally organized, and the parents would troop in to take their seats. At a signal from someone inside, the large, metal door opened, and soon Jackson was shuffling his way inside with the others.

He was surprised to find a full theatre-style auditorium behind the doors. This was no high school gym.

"It's where they hold the government and politics classes," Courtney whispered to him, noticing his confusion.

"We've got one like this in my school too," added MacKenzie.

Shrugging, he followed his wife and daughter to their assigned seats, noting that at least his seat was padded and more comfortable than a gym bench would have been. Once seated, he had time to check out his surroundings.

The seats were arranged in ascending rows, giving everyone a good view. They faced a large, deep stage that was bathed in bright light. A large picture of President Meyers formed the backdrop to the stage, the portrait lit with spotlights. In front of the picture, rows of chairs were arranged facing outwards, and then in front of those, a podium.

Just as he was about to whisper something to his wife, music started and the entire audience rose to their feet. It was not the national anthem, but a march that had been composed in honor of the presidential birthday, and had become a popular patriotic song for occasions like this.

His heart swelling with pride, Jackson watched as row after row of the graduating high school class walked onto the stage, standing in lines next to the arranged seats. All were dressed the same in the simple gray and white uniform that marked them as high school students. MacKenzie wore an identical uniform, as was required of her at any formal occasion, though hers, of course, had a slightly different insignia on the shoulder as she attended a different school. What a difference it made, Jackson thought, to see teenagers looking neat and tidy rather than slouching around in jeans and sneakers. Courtney had been ambivalent about the decision to clothe students in uniforms, and the girls had been absolutely livid, but Jackson thought that the decision had been a good one. Everyone looked like they belonged, and there was no difference based on socioeconomic status or tastes in music. He approved, but as a military man he could be expected to.

As the music ended, the audience and the students resumed their seats, and Jackson waited as a tall, elegant looking man took to the stage. He was familiar with the principal, and remained quiet, as did everyone else, waiting for the official start of the ceremony.

"Ladies and gentlemen, friends, parents, relatives and students," began the principal. "Please rise for our national anthem."

This was expected. Every formal occasion these days began with the anthem, and Jackson got to his feet and sang along with practiced ease. The old anthem that Jackson remembered from his childhood was long gone. Singing about the Stars and Stripes was considered to be insulting to those that had joined the country under the new flag. Instead, the old anthem had been replaced by "Praises to Our President," a song that Jackson had first heard at Maya's sixth grade graduation, though it had not yet been elevated to anthem at the time. After the full eight verses, the audience remained standing for the Pledge, which Jackson remembered with a grin had been such a shock to him the first time he heard it. Now, though, it was second nature, and he reeled it off without a pause.

Technicalities taken care of, the business of graduation was quickly attended to. The salutatorian spoke, followed by the valedictorian, both choosing to thank the president for his influence on their education. The principal also spoke, again commenting on the positive ways in which changes to educational policy had affected the graduating class, and expressing his wish that all should become good and faithful citizens of the UCSA.

Jackson was wriggling a little in his seat by now, the speeches having gone on for what seemed like hours. Both Courtney and MacKenzie were watching silently, paying attention and following every word. Perhaps, Jackson thought, it was because he saw the president in person nearly every day that he was not quite as enmeshed in the cult of the leader as everyone else seemed to be. He respected Meyers, certainly, but knew that the man wasn't a God. Yet none of what he was seeing here today was new to him. He'd been to many such public occasions and all were the same. He supposed that the love of the people was what came along with great leadership, and many of these students remembered no one other than Meyers as president. It would be a long time before any of them knew another leader. Meyers' position as leader had been ratified by a unanimous cabinet earlier this year, and he would hold the position as long as the country was under threat.

It had seemed fair at the time, since no one wanted the upheaval of elections, and besides, the opening of voting booths was still deemed to be a danger to the public. It had all made sense and was explained with such clear logic that Jackson would have had to have been a fool to disagree with the move. Despite this, there was something under the elementary logic that didn't sit well with him, like he had forgotten something. Ever since he'd read Maya's book, the words of Franklin had echoed around his head and, try as he might, he just couldn't forget them.

Finally, the principal was announcing the names of the graduates. As each student came up to receive his or her diploma, the audience applauded, and Jackson did too. He saved up his loudest cheers for his beautiful daughter, who gave him a wide, cheeky grin as she faced him from the stage.

When the diplomas had been given out and the students had returned to their seats, the principal gave the signal for everyone to once again rise to their feet. They did so, and the students stood and turned so that they were facing the portrait of Meyers that had been behind them. Then, with a loud, raucous cheer they removed their graduation hats and with a shout of "Long Live Meyers" tossed them into the air to the great delight and noisy approval of all gathered.

It was only when the beaming student faces turned back to their parents that Jackson noticed Maya's cap sitting firmly on her head. She must have found it quickly, he thought, or probably just caught it after she tossed it; she'd always been coordinated.

He was smiling, beaming, so proud of his little girl, and he put his arm around Courtney's shoulder and held MacKenzie's hand as the new graduates marched off the stage. This was happiness, he thought. They'd head out for ice cream after this, as family tradition dictated, and then he had something special for Maya. He wanted to give her a gift as a reward for all her hard work. His little girl was all grown up.

Later that evening, Jackson held the small pink box in his hand. It had taken him months to procure this gift for Maya, and he was going to make sure that she got it even though he had a horrible feeling that he was doing the wrong thing. She was going to love it so much that he couldn't help himself. So why was he nervous? It had been an arduous task for him to find what he was holding in such a small box, the size of the box not giving away the importance of what lay inside it. Inside the box was none other than an old American flag lapel pin—the Stars and Stripes. Maya was obsessed with learning about the revolutionary war and all the information she could get her hands on about the old United States of America. It was a passion that he himself had created by accident, and he regretted it to this day. While it wasn't exactly banned to have information about the USA—nothing was exactly banned—it certainly was frowned upon to be seen reading about the country that used to be. However, Maya loved all that old historical stuff. His patriotism had created hers, and she had loved it because of him. He had given her a book, *Johnny Tremain*, that his father had read to him, one of the only pleasant memories that he had of his father. When her dad was gone, Maya read it to feel closer to him.

The book had been a present that was both thoughtful and thoughtless, but, Jackson thought, he couldn't have known what would come of it. Maya fell in love with old history, wanting to collect anything she could about the original country. Such artifacts were becoming more and more difficult to find. Memorabilia of the old country had been destroyed or lost to time. There was a new motto to their world, one that dictated that they should look to the future and leave the past behind.

History wasn't popular anymore. It was still taught in school with a focus on the recent present and little mention beyond glossing over the 1500–2050 range. The books made the pilgrims sound like adventure-seekers rather than individuals seeking religious freedom, and the founding fathers were not even mentioned by name. Maybe Maya heard the missing pieces that her school books left behind. She loved history—couldn't get enough of it. He'd consoled himself with the thought that, under certain circumstances studying history was allowed. If you were to be a government teacher, for example, knowing the old history was important so that it could be refuted. Only the most loyal were allowed to become that kind of teacher.

Maya spent money buying books on the black market, books that he had occasionally lent her money for, thinking that if he indulged her, she'd grow out of the phase. She had hidden relics of an old, forgotten past under her bed, including an old novelty copy of the constitution. It wasn't common to have the old constitution without its modern counterpart standing next to it as evidence that the world had moved on and grown bigger and better, so he told her to only take it out when she was alone in her room.

The Apocalytes, he thought, had ruined it for everyone. The quasi-religious sect that had grown up around the horrific events of July 14th, 2051 had, for a while, been a force to be reckoned with as more and more people joined, looking for an explanation for what had been brought down on their great nation. Their numbers had waned, of course, over time, but they were still around.

A large part of the Apocalytes' belief system centered on the fact that the country as it stood was illegal because it had not ratified the original constitution before adopting a new one. Therefore the new constitution was a flawed document that held no authority over them. The Apocalytes had highjacked history for their own means, and made it all about their weird beliefs. They went around claiming that the world was about to end, and that the making of so-called mega countries like the UCSA was a sure sign that the end was near. Jackson snorted to himself at the thought of it.

What was more concerning for him, though, was that the Apocalytes had used their knowledge of old history to further their cause. There had been sympathy for the Apocalytes at the beginning, though most wanted them gone. After the assassination of the Mexican president and the formation of the UCSA, things changed. People no longer had patience for fringe groups, least of all for a fringe group that thought the president and his work were sure signs of the end.

At that time, everything the Apocalytes associated themselves with became taboo. People shunned history and old America simply because of the Apocalytes, rather than any government ban. For a while, people had continued to celebrate old American holidays like Thanksgiving, but before long, these associations with the Apocalytes meant that the popularity of such holidays diminished in favor of more patriotic days like Memorial Day and UCSA Day.

There were other fringe groups, of course, like the Sons of Freedom, but even they were seen as related to the Apocalytes and therefore shunned. The study of history became less and less important, and people began to worry about the present and insecure future that the news channels consistently discussed. The original US history class became an elective and was replaced with

UCSA history. It was one elective that Maya had taken with brisk and cheerful readiness. Most school history classes went back only as far as the founding of the North American Union anyway, so Jackson had seen no harm in letting his daughter take them. Books and information weren't banned so they were still available in libraries for those interested in that sort of thing, but few people borrowed them and even fewer purchased the dusty copies that were available for sale.

The constitution was an even dodgier subject, and one that made Jackson slightly afraid for his daughter. People would say "remember Rick Baker," and he would. Baker, a former Chicago councilman, had been photographed showing off a prized possession, which had turned out to be a copy of the Bill of Rights. Not frightening, or even illegal, in itself, but what happened next was.

Jackson knew this story intimately as he had family in Chicago, some of whom happened to live in Baker's neighborhood, so he'd heard about the events first-hand. It had been a warm summer day two years ago with children playing in the streets and dads grilling in the backyards. Everyone had, of course, seen the pictures of Rick in the local tabloid articles. It was definitely him, though a young Baker, one who hadn't yet started balding or developed the spare tire around his middle that he had these days. He was right there on the cover of the tabloids holding what was described as the Bill of Rights, wearing a yellow plaid button down shirt and khakis, grinning from ear to ear.

People in the neighborhood didn't like this, to be sure, but it seemed innocent enough and the picture looked old anyway. Some thought it was a joke or even a similar-looking relative of Rick's. Baker himself was well known as a prankster, always pulling gags around the neighborhood, despite his elevated position in local government. What he thought was funny was not necessarily what anyone else thought of as funny, but people put up with him because having a friend in the government was useful. Just being nice to him and laughing at his jokes was the only payment that he seemed to require for favors.

So on that fine almost-perfect day filled with the smell of charcoal and children's laughter, strangers had begun throwing rotten food at Rick's home as they drove by. The media incited the general populace, apart from the neighborhood, of course, to portray Baker as a raving lunatic member of the fringe. There was speculation about whether he was a Son of Freedom or a more serious Apocalyte. If he were found to be a member of either, there would be serious consequences: people didn't deal with fringe political groups anymore.

Although none of these consequences were nearly as bad as what would happen if speculation began that Baker was a member of Hariq Jihad, of course. If such speculation began, he'd be condemned as a terrorist long before any evidence could be presented. He faced possible arrest. At minimum, he would have to give up his job and probably move out of the neighborhood as well. Whether or not you were a terrorist was far less important than the appearance of guilt. If someone thought you were a terrorist, then that was enough to be convicted in the public's eye.

Luckily for Baker, it didn't look as if things were going that way for him. He was being touted as a bit of a lunatic and a member of a fringe political group but nothing worse. There was a lot of public speculation of how old that picture was, but it didn't seem to matter in the end, at least not to anyone except Rick Baker himself. However, no one was listening to what he had to say.

As everyone was enjoying the sunny weather outside, some noticed a black car speeding through the neighborhood and thought to themselves, How dangerous, to be speeding like that with kids around. That car was not half as dangerous as the Molotov cocktail that sailed through the air a little later, launched from the black car and aimed directly at the Baker house.

It was terrifying but quick thinking prevailed. Many people in the neighborhood helped Baker and his family, though some stood back to watch the show. The fire department was called and the Baker home was saved with minimal damage. Despite the aid of the neighbors that day, he'd lost all political clout, and the reactions of his neighbors had more to do with fear for their neighborhood than a will to help a pariah.

Later that night, when everyone was sleeping, the Bakers disappeared. This was the first family that Jackson had heard of this happening to. When he first heard the story, he didn't believe it, preferring to believe the Baker's ran away, moving to a town that didn't know or recognize Rick. Logically, Jackson knew better. The Bakers left everything behind, including suitcases and all their clothes. They were simply gone. Their home left vacant, their car in the driveway where it always was, and the keys on the hook by the door. The house was left there locked after the initial police search, waiting for something or someone. People in the neighborhood wanted the area to look nice so they took to mowing his lawn and collecting his mail until, as many guessed, the post office put an indefinite hold on it.

It was a mystery. The Bakers were gone long enough that people forgot exactly what he was supposed to have done, and they became genuinely worried for the family. You could look through the windows of their home and see everything exactly as they'd left it. Clothes were scattered over the floor, and the place was in disarray, far from the clean and orderly home that Mrs. Baker usually kept. It was like the Bakers had ceased to exist, and the neighborhood kids were left to come up with fantastical stories about what had happened to them that became stranger and stranger as time went on.

Some thought that the Bakers had been kidnapped and murdered by the same people who had thrown the Molotov cocktail that had done little more than scorch the front porch. Others thought that the Bakers had left under cover of night to give their lives to the Apocalytes. No one knew for sure because no one heard from them.

It wasn't until many months later, in the midst of the hot 2079 autumn, that Rick Baker, his wife and his teenage son returned to the neighborhood. At the time, Jackson was there in person, visiting family as the girls were on autumn vacation from the now year-round school. All three Bakers looked like you could see right through them, ghosts of their former selves. They had lost weight, but it seemed as if they'd lost substance as well, looking pale, gray and lifeless.

They returned just as they had left, in the middle of the night. Rick Baker came out in the middle of the afternoon the following day to try start the car in the driveway. After sitting idle for so long, of course, the car wouldn't start. It needed a jump, and Jackson watched through the window of his cousin's house as Rick sat in the car, trying again and again to turn the engine over. It looked like no one was about to help, and taking pity on the man, Jackson went to the garage, grabbed a set of jumper cables and walked across the street.

"Hey, need a hand?" he asked cheerfully as he got close to the car.

Rick Baker looked up, an expression of fear on his face that cleared only when he saw the jumper cables in Jackson's hands.

"Yes, please," he said, his voice barely a whisper.

Jackson attached the cables and brought his own car over, and within ten minutes Rick's car was humming softly in the driveway.

"There you go," said Jackson. "All set."

"Thank you," said Baker. His voice cracked.

"You alright?" asked Jackson, suddenly concerned about the man.

Baker looked up at him, his eyes blank and nodded.

"Just wanted to get back here for the kid," he mumbled.

Jackson didn't understand what he meant, but didn't especially want to hang around and find out, so he just nodded. He grabbed his cables, threw them on the passenger seat of his car and drove back across the street. By the time he'd parked again, Baker was gone.

Later that night, Rick Baker hung himself in the garage of his home. His wife and son left the neighborhood shortly after, and no one heard of them again.

That was why he was so worried about his daughter. Keeping the constitution under your bed might not be illegal, but it could bring down a whole heap of trouble. Despite all this, he encouraged her. Again he looked at the little pink box in his hand, uncertain whether he should give it to her.

It couldn't hurt. He knew his girl, and she wasn't an Apocalyte or anything like it. She just had a curious and enquiring mind. She'd be starting college soon and was sure to grow out of all this stuff as she studied, was challenged more, and made new friends. It was such a small thing. It would be the last, he promised himself; this would be his last gift of this kind. Anyway, it had been very difficult to get a hold of. He remembered with a shiver the thrill of finding the pin.

He'd been searching for weeks for the perfect graduation gift for Maya. Nothing he'd seen was quite right. It was late one night while he was surfing the internet, looking for inspiration, that he found a website dedicated to old history. It was not illegal, though he did switch to a private internet browser before he opened it. He'd been looking for books to give her, maybe a first edition of one of her favorites, but had stumbled on this instead. At the bottom of the page was a link to classified ads.

Looking over his shoulder and then feeling foolish, Jackson had read through the ads. When he'd seen the pin, he'd known immediately that it was the absolute perfect present for his daughter. Even better, this wasn't a private sale; there was some kind of shop that he could go to with an address.

He'd considered his decision for a week before telling Courtney that he was working late to drive over to a district of DC that he wasn't familiar with at all. He'd been careful to wear sports gear rather than his normal suit, with a baseball hat pulled over his head. He kept his service weapon on him just in case, and he'd parked his car streets away. When he got to the listed address, he found it was nothing more than a liquor store.

Half relieved that he didn't have to go through with something questionable, and half disappointed that he hadn't managed to get the perfect present, he wondered what the hell he was supposed to do now. At that moment, a police cruiser turned the corner and without even thinking, Jackson dived into the liquor store. He hadn't done anything, but he didn't want to look suspicious, so liquor it was. He wandered the aisle and figured that he'd pick up a bottle of something nice to take home, like a good whiskey to drink on the deck.

Bottle chosen, he'd gone to the cash desk where a thin, young man, bearded and wearing a dirty t-shirt was sitting. He placed the bottle on the counter.

"That all?" asked the man.

"Um, yes," said Jackson. If he'd wanted anything else, he'd have chosen it, surely.

"You sure?" the guy asked.

Suddenly it dawned on Jackson that a store selling American memorabilia was hardly likely to just be sitting out in the open. It'd be firebombed in no time. This had to be a front.

"How'd you know?" he asked.

The man shrugged. "You're all dressed up for covert activities with nowhere to go," he said. "This all ain't illegal, you know."

"I know," said Jackson, sheepishly.

Technically, it wasn't. It was still black market, and he knew it. There wasn't going to be sales tax paid. He knew that shops such as this were unlikely to be on the up and up. Regardless, he told the man what he was looking for, saw the goods and paid a healthy amount of cash for what he now held in this little pink box.

He had left the store, heart beating hard against his ribs. As he held the box in his pocket, remaining aware of his surroundings, he heard someone start yelling. Breaking into a run, he turned onto the next street, but the yelling grew closer until he gave up, knowing he wasn't faster in these unfamiliar streets than whoever was behind him.

"You forgot this," said the store clerk, through gasping breaths.

He was holding out the bottle of whiskey and Jackson began to laugh. He laughed until there were tears in his eyes, all the way back to his car.

Now, here he was, with the perfect gift in hand. He was going to give it to Maya, he decided. He would also make it perfectly clear that this was the last of things like this, and that there would be no more collecting, no more discussions. She was a grown up now, and she had to grow out of this phase. That, he decided, was the best thing to do.

It was exactly what he did. And the smile on Maya's face when she opened the box made it all worthwhile.

13

THE SIXTH YEAR

February 19th, 2081
Jackson Home, Alexandria, Virginia, UCSA
Article Originally Published in the *Union Standard*, special President's Day edition, Reused with Permission
President Meyers: Champion of the American Republic?
Gerrard Montangna, Political Editor

On this, the day that we celebrate the most important and powerful of people, it seems like a reminder is in order. While we may, in the past, have glorified those who built our nation, those who wrote laws and enacted rules, those who fought tyrants and defeated great powers to bring us independence, it seems that now is a time to appreciate what we have, and what we will have. This country, the grand United Continental States of America, owes everything down to its very existence to one man.

Thirty years ago, our nation was decimated by a series of attacks that killed thousands—attacks on our own soil that were unprovoked, unnecessary, and insane. Not a day goes by that we're not reminded of this in even the smallest of ways. The body scanning devices that you take your child through on the way to school. The travel permission that you need to go one state over. Everything our country has become owes itself in some way to what this terrorist group did to us. A group that I will not even grant the respect of naming.

It may be easy for critics to look at that and ask, what have we become? But we need a reminder of what we have really become. The UCSA is a country with close to zero unemployment levels, unlike the United Kingdom. There is no religious warfare on our soil, as in France. Our citizens have access to the best healthcare in the globe, and all for free, unlike in China where only those who can pay are treated. There is no homelessness, unlike in many South American countries. When it comes to basic needs, we are not only taken care of, we are fortunate. Our constantly growing economy means we live lives of luxury, drive nice cars, eat big meals, and yet there is one more thing that we have that many don't.

The UCSA is safe. We do not live in fear. We do not worry about sending our children to school, about leaving our sleeping wives in bed, about walking the streets at night. Since the founding of the UCSA, there has not been one single successful terrorist attack on UCSA soil. Not one innocent person has lost their lives due to terrorism. How many countries in the world can say that? I'll tell you the answer: none.

And the all-important reminder? All of this, every single fact, is down to one man: President Frederick J. Meyers.

Meyers has served tirelessly for far longer than his original term to bring this country to a state of stability, safety and security. Day after day, he has performed this thankless task, so focused on creating a haven for the civilian population that he has even agreed to continue in his position indefinitely. Without thought for himself, his family, or his personal needs, he continues to serve our country and to make it the greatest nation that the world has ever seen.

So, on this day, this day of presidents, when we might be tempted to look to the past, I urge you instead to look to today. Look at the man that represents our great nation and bow. Is President Meyers the champion of the American republic? You bet. But he's also our savior, our protector and our leader. We would be nothing without him, and are everything with him, and that is the true meaning of today. If you have any doubt about this, then simply ask yourself where we would be without him. And then rid yourself of all your doubt.

■ ■ ■

Maya was out. Though she was in college now, it had been decided that she would still live at home. It was easier that way, and she still had access to the best universities in the country. Probably it was a good thing that she had stayed, Jackson thought, as he put down his tablet. He'd been waiting until the house was quiet, waiting so that he could do something that was uncomfortable and yet necessary, but something that he didn't want anyone else to see.

Where was Maya? He had no idea. Hanging out with friends maybe? She never spoke much about what she was doing anymore. Since she'd graduated high school, she'd grown quieter, more secretive. She came and went as she pleased, never saying where she was going or who she was with. For a while, Jackson had come down on her like a ton of bricks every time she came home, telling her that she was disrespecting his house. Courtney had calmed him, reminding him that their daughter was an adult now, and that she had the right to a little privacy.

Maybe she did, he'd thought, but now he was about to invade that privacy. He'd suspected for a while that she was up to something. She didn't talk to him like his little girl used to. Ever since he'd given her the graduation present and told her that it was the last, that she needed to leave this obsession with history behind, it was like they had no connection anymore. She began speaking more and more like one of those crazy Apocalytes about obscure ideas, liberty and freedom. Freedom, he thought, was fine. He was an American, freedom was what he fought for, but freedom from terrorism was the goal, not freedom to run around doing whatever the hell you liked. Besides, any other kind of freedom was just unnecessary, as everything else was taken care of. The UCSA was a great country, and he believed that. It was full of people who cared about everyone's well-being and who wanted them to succeed.

There was something going on here; he could feel it. He no longer tried to kid himself that this was a phase of Maya's, though in his heart he still hoped that it was. Whatever it was had gone on long enough. She still lived at home, and she could be putting all of them at risk if she was up to something. He would have none of that under his watch.

He had determined that he was going to search her room. They had attempted to give her the independence and privacy she deserved as an adult. They had left her room alone, let her have her little sanctuary, but enough was enough. He felt bad about invading her space, but at the same time knew it was necessary. It was his job to protect his family. He had reasonable cause to break his trust with his daughter, he reasoned, if only to protect her from herself. That was all that really mattered to Jackson: protecting his daughter and his family. Protection was extremely important in this world, protection from terrorists, but also protection from oneself.

Slowly, feeling older than he'd felt for a long time, Jackson pulled himself up out of his chair. He took a moment to take a deep breath. He was, he realized, afraid of finding something, and also afraid of finding nothing and having broken his daughter's trust for no reason. There was no putting it off; he needed to do this.

He walked down the narrow hallway, past pictures of his daughters that chronicled their lives. Wide-eyed babies turned into grinning toddlers, gap toothed elementary school kids, then gawky teenagers until there were two, beautiful young women. He felt the urge to cry. Where had all those years gone? They'd all seemed to just slip through his fingers, eluding him whenever he tried to grasp at them. In that moment, he regretted every second that he'd spent away from them all: every heartbeat that he'd missed, every minute he hadn't been there, away from his wife and his daughters, busy fighting another man's war. In the end, he had done it for them. He had been brave and sacrificed of himself for their happiness and protection. That was what he was doing now, he reminded himself. He just needed to be sure, needed to know, and then... Well, he'd deal with that when he knew.

He turned the doorknob to Maya's room. They'd never had locks on the doors, working on trust instead, and he had a sick feeling as he betrayed that trust, but he continued anyway. He pushed the door open, hearing it slide against the carpet at the bottom. He inhaled sharply and forced all the air from his lungs as he walked in.

Everything seemed so familiar—the outlines of trophies and dolls that he'd known for years. He looked around, wanting to touch everything in sight. There was still so much of this room that screamed 'daddy's little girl.' He wanted to sit on her bed and sob. He wanted to go back to when things were much simpler, when he could solve her problems with a hug and a kiss.

He flicked on the light, wanting to see better what it was he was doing. He could see nothing unexpected, but then anything incriminating would hardly be out in the open, now would it? Jackson cursed himself for thinking of his daughter as a criminal.

Going to the desk, he slid open drawers to find everything neatly stacked inside, nothing strange. The bookshelf held nothing that he hadn't seen before. There was nothing under the bed, and no hidden cupboards or niches where anything could be hidden. The weight in his stomach was beginning to lift. He'd been wrong—he'd misjudged her and he felt bad about that, but he'd deal with his guilt. He'd found nothing.

As he was about to leave the room, heart skipping in his chest, he had one more thought. Turning, he lifted up a corner of the mattress, finding, as he'd known he would, the novelty copy of the old American constitution. He smiled a little, not believing that Maya had really kept this, but maybe it had sentimental meaning. He was about to put the mattress back down when he caught a glimpse of green, almost ignored it, but then thought, What the hell? Pushing the heavy mattress up a little further, he groped under it and came out with a book.

His legs gave way under him, making him sink to the carpet, the book still in his hands. He read the words again and again, not believing them, knowing that they weren't true but knowing that they had to be. The book was *The Federalist Papers*, by Alexander Hamilton, James Madison, and John Jay. This book had a far more ominous meaning today; it was otherwise known as the Apocalyte Bible. Jackson's stomach turned and his blood became ice water. He hadn't been wrong.

The cool summer air blew through the house and it was late. Jackson was sitting out on the deck, waiting for the click of the front door, wondering what the hell he was supposed to do. An empty glass stood on the arm of his chair. He'd had a drink, just one, but he'd needed it. The deck wrapped around the side of the house so he had a view of the street from here. He glanced up occasionally from his phone. He was playing a game, something like Tetris, only harder. It helped keep him awake, helped stop him from thinking, but it also frustrated him.

There was still, he guessed, a chance that he could be wrong. He tried to be reasonable, tried to give her the benefit of the doubt. Perhaps the book belonged to someone else or she had stumbled on it, not realizing what it meant. Those were lies, and he knew it. Still, he couldn't help but hope. He had no idea what the hell he was supposed to do.

Maya slept much of the day and was out most of the night, leaving the house to go to night classes, and then disappearing off, allegedly with her friends. He wondered what could possibly require so much time from her, though he supposed that now at least he had an inkling. He hadn't raised his daughter to be like this, hadn't sacrificed everything so that she could turn out this way. He wanted her to go to school, go to college, get a job, get married, have kids, be happy. He didn't raise her to be so...aimless. Aimless was a dangerous thing these days—it was exactly what the Apocalytes looked for in young recruits, what drew them to people. Replacing that aimlessness with religious fervor was easy.

After finding the book, he needed to make sure that Maya wasn't doing anything really stupid. Reading banned material was fine as long as she didn't get caught. Having contact with Apocalytes to obtain such reading material was still okay with

Jackson. Well, not fine, but he could deal with it. He just had to reassure himself that she wasn't doing more than that, though he didn't really think she was. He'd raised her with such belief, such loyalty, that he honestly didn't think she'd be able to go against everything that she'd been taught. But he had to be sure.

Glancing up again, he saw her coming up the block and put down his phone. Her long, flowing dress brushed against the ground. Her hair, dark like her mother's, was braided, bouncing against her back as she moved. She was walking, as she often did, which was seen as odd by some. No one walked much these days with self-driving cars, but Maya did. She said that it helped her think, though maybe, Jackson thought, that wasn't a good thing. If she had a little less time to think, maybe she wouldn't get into so much trouble. Could that be the problem? He'd let her think too much?

He stood up so that she could see him as she walked towards the house. When she caught sight of him, she hesitated for a moment, then hurriedly pushed something inside her bag before slowly walking up the outside deck steps.

"What are you hiding?" he asked, the secretive motion making him suspicious, making his voice gruff and annoyed.

Maya, who had been half way to smiling at her father, turned defensive, putting an arm over her stuff. "Nothing," she snapped, all traces of a smile gone now. "It's none of your business."

"It is my damn business when you come home late," he snapped back, already regretting that he was losing his temper but unable to stop himself. "It's nearly three in the morning," he continued. "I've been waiting here for you all night."

"No one told you to wait here for me all night, Dad," Maya sighed, shaking her head and rolling her eyes at the stupidity of adults, even though she was close to being one herself. She stared him down for a moment and then deemed the conversation over, crossing her arms and moving towards the house.

"Don't you walk away from me," he growled through gritted teeth. "I want to see what you've got in that bag of yours."

"No," she said, truculently, for she could be as stubborn and hard-headed as her father. "It's none of your business, I've already told you."

"Give me the bag," Jackson said, and reaching out, grabbed for it.

For a ridiculous moment, they tussled, father and daughter, over the cotton bag, before it slipped from Maya's shoulder and Jackson found himself in full possession of it. Quickly, he opened it, rifling through the contents inside and ignoring the usual make-up bag, phone, and keys until he found a paper, a pamphlet that he pulled out and looked at in the dim light.

'Liberty Now' was written on the front cover.

Apocalytes, he thought, and felt his stomach sink—Apocalytes. Even in that moment, he could see her goodness and still love her because she hadn't fulfilled his largest unspoken fear: she wasn't a terrorist.

"So you've become a cultist, then?" he said, bitterly, screwing the pamphlet up in his hand.

Maya bit her lip and shook her head. "No, Daddy," she said. "It's not like that."

He was struck by the word daddy. She never called him that anymore, and it soothed him, just a little, as maybe she had meant it to do.

"Then what is it like?" he asked, more softly.

"Look," said Maya, trying to be reasonable, but looking a little afraid that they could be overheard. "Can we do this inside?"

Jackson nodded, and they went into the house, closing the door behind them. He stood with his arms crossed, expectant of an immediate explanation. He wasn't going to be deterred.

"We're not religious nuts," Maya said, turning to him. "We're trying to do something good for the country, return it back to the principles that once made this a great nation."

Her voice was logical and calm. Jackson shook his head. "Oh, God," was all he could say.

"We aren't nuts," repeated Maya, beginning to look stubborn and annoyed again.

"You..." Jackson's voice cracked and was so quiet that he could hardly believe that it was his own, but then he could hardly believe what he was about to say. He cleared his throat and tried again. "You're talking open rebellion on our country."

"I'm talking about returning it back to our country," Maya said. "Think about it. When was the last time we had an election? We're supposed to be a great democracy, except we're not a democracy anymore, are we? We're a dictatorship with that creep Meyers at the helm."

Trying to be as reasonable as his daughter was being, trying to match her on her own ground rather than losing his temper again, Jackson put his hand on her arm and said, "He's the good guy, honey, trust me; I know him. He wants only what's best. And we don't need elections while we're busy fighting terrorism. We don't have time for them, and we don't have the security forces to keep them safe for people. We need to get things secure before we do anything drastic."

"And when will that be?" Maya asked, raising a questioning eyebrow, but sounding sarcastic, which riled Jackson again. "When will things be secure, Dad? They need to fix this now.

We need to go back to being a government for the people and by the people."

"No!" Jackson yelped, his temper slipping out of his control again.

From down the hall, a light flickered on, and there was the sound of footsteps over the sound of Jackson's ragged breathing.

"What's going on?" came Courtney's voice from the corridor. Then her sleepy face turned into the kitchen. "It's three o'clock in the damn morning."

"Oh, nothing," said Jackson, mimicking Maya's sarcasm. "Just that our daughter's an Apocalyte."

Courtney frowned as if trying to take this in through a half haze of sleep. "I'm sure that's not true," she said, doubtfully. "We raised her far better than that."

"Oh no," said Jackson, who had been hoping to keep this from Courtney but through his own anger was now forced to tell her. "It's true. And even worse than that, she's standing right here in our kitchen and talking open sedition."

"Wait, what?"

Courtney looked at her daughter, trying to get a sense of just what the hell was going on.

"Ma," sighed Maya. "It's not that serious. I'm not talking about killing anyone or anything. All I was saying is that the country needs to go back to the basics, the founding principles, if you will."

Courtney's eyes widened. "Oh no," she moaned. "Oh no."

"Oh no indeed," agreed Jackson.

"Go to your room," Courtney said, abruptly. Not able to process this all at once, she fell back on what had worked so well when Maya had been a child.

"I'm a grown woman," Maya declared.

"Go to your room," demanded Courtney, again.

Maya gave a theatrical sigh and then picked up her bag. "Fine," she said.

They waited until they heard her door slam before Courtney turned back to Jackson.

"What are we going to do, Ant?" she asked, pitifully. "What are we going to do?"

"I don't know, I really don't," Jackson said. "She's a radical. How the hell did she turn out like this?" He was still angry, holding on to his temper by a thread.

"We didn't raise her to be like this," Courtney said sadly.

"I'll talk some sense in her tomorrow," he told her.

"But what if she gets arrested? What if she disappears like the Jamisons? What if we all disappear?" Courtney was panicking now, becoming hysterical.

Jackson took charge. "She won't, we won't," he said, taking his wife by the arm. "She's not Hariq Jihad, and according to her, she's not even an Apocalyte. Maybe it's not as serious as it seems at first glance. I'll talk sense into her tomorrow, and we'll see where we go from there. But right now there's nothing you can do, Court, so let's get you back to bed."

He escorted her back to the bedroom, got her into bed and went into the master bathroom. Pulling a package of pills from the cupboard, he pushed out two sleeping pills and poured a glass of water, taking them into the bedroom for Courtney before going to get ready for bed himself. She was already sleeping by the time he crawled in next to her.

What the hell was he going to do?, he wondered as he lay back on his pillow in the dark room. Maybe he could talk to someone at work about it. Not tell them the whole truth, of course, but maybe get some advice. Perhaps they had some kind of light rehabilitation program for those that weren't quite indoctrinated yet—a reminder of what made this country great.

He could try keep her hidden away in the house. He could un-brainwash her himself. He was a smart military man who had rallied people to the cause of his country; he could damn well do the same for his daughter. If she spent enough time away from whoever these nuts were that she was hanging out with, then she'd be back to his beautiful little girl again. She'd go back to being happy and stop all this ridiculous talk.

It was his job, he reminded himself, to protect his family. That is what he would do. If anyone else found out about the kind of things that Maya was saying, there was no telling what would happen. Who could he trust with that kind of information? It was when you started trusting people with secrets that those secrets got out. The obvious solution was to keep this in the family. He wondered if it would be possible to keep the secret even from MacKenzie. He could maybe say that Maya was sick, which in truth she was.

Outside, a car drove down the street, the light from its headlights sweeping across the bedroom ceiling. Jackson's heart caught in his throat. He didn't breathe normally again until the car drove past the house and continued on its way. This, he finally knew, was what it was like to live in fear—to live in fear that the car outside your house was coming to make you and your beloved family disappear. No longer would he assume that a passing car was someone going to work early or innocently coming home from a party. There would be a constant sense of danger.

If he turned Maya in, and that is what it would be—turning her in—there was every chance that he, Courtney and MacKenzie would never have to live in fear. If he kept Maya at home, he was going to stop breathing every time a car passed the house in the night. He only had one chance to get this right, one chance to make the best decision. What a decision it was.

Maya was his little girl, his baby, his angel. He thought back to the way her little chubby arms and legs would wriggle in delight when he picked her up as a baby. Then he had given her that damn book, that stupid book that his drunken father had read to him as a child, and all this had begun. She was his life, his flesh and blood, and no matter what she did he would always love her. He would never abandon her, even if that meant increasing the danger to the rest of the family. Besides, the survivors wouldn't forgive him.

He'd keep her at home; it was the only way to do things. She was reasonable and intelligent. He'd be able to talk sense into her, even if it took a few weeks. Then all would be fine; they'd all be fine. This would be over and they could go on with their happy little lives.

At the back of his mind, a little voice nagged at him. What if this didn't work? What if he couldn't get her to see the error of her ways? What if someone, somewhere, already knew about her, already knew where she lived? So many what ifs...

14

THE SEVENTH YEAR

January 14th, 2082
The White House, Washington DC, UCSA
Article Originally Published in the *Toronto Star*, Reused
with Permission
Alberta Police Raid Apocalyte Headquarters
Barry D'Amico, Crime Reporter

Late last night, under cover of darkness, Alberta police launched a daring raid on a safe house believed to be the headquarters of the province's Apocalyte sect. Three teams of officers, under the command of Captain Edward J. Larson, raided the split level home in an undisclosed suburban location.

According to Larson, the raid was a complete success, ending with the arrest and detainment of no less than thirty dissenters, the seizing of several boxes worth of seditious material, and the destruction of the building itself. It is as yet unclear how many of the arrested were known dissenters.

The raid was part of a nationwide scheme under new articles added to the National Defense Act just last week, which give police increased powers to search and seize locations thought to be connected to the Apocalytes. The president amended the National Defense Act in response to public pressure to end the ongoing protests and occasional violence enacted by the religious sect.

Though Apocalytes have been in existence since 2051, it is only recently that their activities have come under close scrutiny by the government. As crackdowns on seditious activity and distribution of seditious materials continue, it is hoped that the Apocalytes will be eradicated by late this year. This audacious goal was set by the president himself, and it seems as though Alberta police are responding to his call to arms.

Under new laws, the seditious culprits will be taken to local detention centers where they will have the opportunity to repent of their crimes and apply for rehabilitation. Should no admission of guilt be given, the arrestees will be transported immediately to prisons to serve out a mandatory ten-year sentence. Judicial review of records will now only be carried out for those suspected of seditious activity, while those known to be seditious, such as culprits arrested on Apocalyte property, for example, will be denied this right.

■ ■ ■

Jackson stood by the driver's side door of his car, the news headline screaming at him from the notification on his tablet screen. His hands were sweating as he tried to lock the doors of the black town car, a car he'd bought simply to fit in with the rest of Washington's elite, and his keys fell from his hands. Scrabbling on the cold black top of the parking garage, Jackson cursed the winter cold that made his fingers numb and the keys icy cold. Almost a year had passed and he needed to admit defeat. He had done what he could for his daughter, and now he needed a new plan.

The last few months had seemed to go by so quickly, and he had attempted to get through to his daughter Maya. He had encouraged her to let go of her radical ideas, to try see that this was just a phase, something that all teenagers and young adults went through. He'd spent long nights talking to her, arguing and debating her. He hoped that she would understand that she felt this way now but she couldn't let it ruin her life. He was not going to allow his daughter to throw away her life for something so trivial, as fleeting as this. Nothing he said could dissuade her. There was only so long that he could keep her imprisoned at home without arousing the suspicions of anyone else, so he'd had to let her out, trust that she'd be discrete.

He wondered how the hell it could be this way, how Maya had turned out like this, when her little sister MacKenzie was the absolute opposite. While Maya was busy trying to subvert the system with her Apocalyte ways, MacKenzie was busy working with the Junior Society of the United Continental States of America. The JSUCSA was a group for patriotic young people like MacKenzie, those who were passionate about their country and the way that it was headed. They had pushed for amendments to the National Defense Act, wanting to mobilize against people like the Apocalytes who espoused the idea that the country was not helping her people but was instead serving the president.

Jackson loved both his daughters equally, but sometimes MacKenzie just made things so much easier for him. In fact, he thought, it was often the idea that she was such a good kid that allowed her to fade into the background, unnoticed. Maya was a typical first-born child—headstrong, passionate, and not easily dissuaded from those things that she was passionate about. For a long time, while Jackson was constantly getting on Maya's case about being so rebellious, he had secretly enjoyed the fact that she was so thoughtful and independent. She might be hard to sway, but that meant that she really thought about everything she believed. In the end, look where that had got him.

What everything came down to was that he loved both his daughters and wanted the best for both of them, and that was why he was nervous, getting ready to do something that he thought he'd never do. He was going to break the law and spy on his own country, in a small way, but it was still something that was against his principles. He would do anything for the daughters that he loved so much, and that was why he'd had to make this choice. He had to do this thing for Maya.

He located his keys and stood up again. He inhaled gently while closing his eyes. He tried to center himself in the same way he'd done when he was out on a mission. He used this time to make an effort to truly calm himself, knowing that he could only operate effectively if he was calm. He needed to successfully infiltrate the intelligence division and get some information about his daughter. He figured that this could be done simply by accessing a computer that someone was already logged into. All he needed to do was to find a way to get inside their offices without anyone realizing what he was up to.

That may be easy as well though, he'd thought. He was polite and friendly, and had many friends among the people working in and around the White House. He'd just have to pop in and see one or two of them, make some small talk to have an excuse to be around. Sure, he could probably ask someone to help him, but that hardly seemed like a bright idea. He didn't want to alert anyone, and these days it was tough to know who to trust. He simply needed to tap into a computer himself, hoping that he'd find one logged in and unattended.

What was he looking for? With Maya becoming increasingly radicalized by the moment, he needed to really think about what he could do, and about how much time he had to do it in. He needed to know if his daughter was being watched, if she was already under suspicion.

If she were, then he had no idea what he would do. If she repented of her radicalization, then they would probably leave her alone. If she stopped hanging out with other radicals, then they were unlikely to do anything to her. But he knew that was wishful thinking; there was no way she would repent, just as there was no way that he could stop her doing what she was doing. She'd never give up. That's just the kind of person that she was: the kind of girl that would die for her beliefs—exactly what he was trying to avoid.

People like that always ended up in the same situation—disappeared. They'd be there one day and gone the next. They'd be out of touch with everyone they ever knew, quickly forgotten by members of their community. It was best not to ask questions about them or where they had gone, like Jackson had done with the Jamisons. That was how it worked now. More than that, should Maya be disappeared, then there was always the chance that they could all come under suspicion, meaning MacKenzie's hopes, dreams, and future were just as much at stake as her older sister's.

He was still uncertain as he locked the car and strode purposefully away from it. He didn't know what the right thing to do was, other than that he had to protect his family at all costs. This was the first step: finding out if she was being watched. He'd figure out a way to save his daughter. There was no way that he'd let anything bad happen to her. She was his first-born child, and that was a special bond. He couldn't let her down.

The Jackson House, Alexandria, Virginia, UCSA

Jackson tapped his fingers on the steering wheel as he whistled along to a song on the radio, turning the wheel as he drove into his development. All had gone according to plan. Finding a computer had been easy, and no one had bothered stopping a man with full security ID, and he'd been able to catch up with a couple of old friends in the process, making his visit appear social. The best part was that he had not found one picture of Maya in the intelligence bureau, nor mention of her name. He'd gone back to finish his shift at work after, and it was difficult to keep the smile off his face as he drove home.

Of course, there was now the problem of what to do with Maya, but at least he knew that she wasn't in any immediate danger, and neither was the rest of his family. She was just a little mixed up. Now that he had this information, he was resolved to try talk to her again. At least he didn't need to worry about anything happening to her, or her disappearing, not right now.

"My baby girl is safe," Jackson said to himself, grinning as he pulled up outside the house to a ruckus.

A group of men were standing outside his home, and Courtney was standing on the porch looking like she was crying. What the hell was going on? One of the men turned and Jackson could clearly see that he was wearing an anti-terrorism task force vest over his uniform. MacKenzie was nowhere in sight. He took this all in within seconds. How could this be? How could this be happening to his baby girl? Maya was safe; she wasn't showcased in the intelligence bureau files. There were no records of her in any of their systems and no pictures of her on their boards. At least, there hadn't been that morning, but it was only mid-afternoon now.

Unless...unless it had all been to throw him off the scent? Unless they knew that he was trying to protect his daughter and guessed what he would do. Looking into the computer may have been the worst thing that he could do because they would realize that he was worried, indicating that Maya must be doing something more serious or dangerous than they had suspected. His mind reeled, trying to put all this information in order. He could still save her, though. All he needed to do was pull rank with someone. He was handpicked by the government. He was handpicked by the president, for God's sake. There was no way that he didn't have the influence to help Maya.

He hurriedly unbuckled his seatbelt and fled from the car, slamming the door behind him.

"Stop! What's going on here?"

About half of the ten or so men on his property turned to look at him as he spoke, while the other half went about their business, continuing to talk into their radios, walking in and out of his home, ignoring him. After a brief second, even those who had looked at him turned back to their previous endeavors. Jackson was not used to being ignored.

Courtney was on the porch, still crying, holding her hand to her mouth and wrapping her other arm around her body in a desperate attempt to comfort herself. She was wearing a pair of yoga pants and a loose t-shirt, her hair thrown up in a messy bun. She must have been cleaning when the team had shown up. Glancing around, Jackson could see that half the neighborhood was out watching what was unfolding in his yard and talking to each other. He almost laughed at the thought of all the parties and barbeques this would get them uninvited to. They were going to be pariahs in their own neighborhood. Then he shook himself. Now wasn't the time to be thinking about that. He needed to concentrate on his sweet Maya and on MacKenzie—where were they?

He walked briskly towards the house, more in control now, and was quickly stopped by a man in an anti-terrorism windbreaker. A badge on a lanyard around his neck identified him as Mark Wilson, and he had the clean cut look of a man who was good at his job and enjoyed it.

Jackson straightened up. Assuming an air of authority, in a voice that was booming but still a little shakier than he would have liked, he said, "What the hell is going on here?"

Wilson looked unimpressed. "And who are you?" he asked.

"I'm Anthony Jackson. This is my home." As he said this, Jackson flashed his White House security card at the man, who noted it and nodded.

"Very good," he said. "We're here investigating a situation with your daughters."

Jackson was about to speak but caught himself. Daughters? Plural? What the hell? Surely he didn't need to worry about MacKenzie now, too?

"You know, we're awfully proud of your daughter," Wilson continued. "She's shown such great dedication to her country."

"I'm sorry, what?"

It was all he could say, his mouth hanging half open as he tried to process all this. He had no idea what he was supposed to make of that. Dedication to country? Surely that sounded far more like MacKenzie than it did Maya? As the words sank in, he had an overwhelming feeling of relief. He could relax now, everything was going to be okay. Dedication to country was a good thing.

But wait, he'd said daughter, singular, this time. And why was Courtney crying? There had to be some kind of reason here, some

212 T. T. MICHAEL

kind of logic, but he couldn't figure out what the hell it was. He turned his back on Wilson abruptly and walked over to Courtney.

"What's wrong, honey?" he asked her softly.

Tears were pouring unchecked down her face. He put his hand on her shoulder, needing her to be there for him, needing answers from her.

"Come on, tell me," he said, still speaking gently. "What's going on here?"

"Oh Ant," she said, finally, wailing and putting her arms around him, crying into his shoulder so that he could barely make out the words. "They're taking Maya."

"Taking her where?" he asked, more confused by the second. "I thought this was about MacKenzie." He realized that he had, ever since the word dedication had been mentioned, automatically assumed that everyone was talking about MacKenzie.

"No," sobbed Courtney. "No, you don't understand. She turned Maya in."

Jackson grabbed his wife's shoulders, pushing her away from his body so that he could see her face. "She did what?"

Courtney gulped and took a shaky breath. "MacKenzie turned Maya in to the anti-terrorism task force," she said.

"But why?" Jackson frowned as he realized that he wasn't asking about MacKenzie's motivations; it was more a matter of logic. "Why would this happen? Maya isn't a member of Hariq Jihad; she's not a terrorist."

"I know that," Courtney said, calming a little in the face of her husband's solid presence. "But those new amendments to the National Defense Act... Apocalytes are now listed as members of anti-government groups. Apparently they had someone come to the school and speak to the JSUCSA. MacKenzie told this person about how Maya is always talking about liberty and voting and all kinds of stupidity, all because of the kind of people that she'd be-ing hanging out with."

"How the..." he stammered a little. "How the hell did this hap-pen? Why would MacKenzie do something like this? There has to be some kind of explanation for her turning in her sister."

"That's just the thing," Courtney said. "MacKenzie did it to be a good citizen. She did her duty."

From inside the house, Jackson could hear yelling and scream-ing. Leaving Courtney on the porch, he walked over the threshold of his home and looked around. To his left, he could see men standing outside Maya's bedroom door. In the kitchen, MacKenzie was sitting calmly at the table, drinking a glass of water and talk-ing to someone who looked in charge. Jackson walked into the kitchen. There was little he could do now, he thought, but maybe he could convince these men that Maya was just a little misguided.

"You need a warrant!" screamed Maya at the top of her lungs from her bedroom.

"Sir, are you the father of this fine young lady?" asked the well-built man sitting at the kitchen table, ignoring the screams from the bedroom.

He was obviously military background, Jackson could tell from his bearing. As he neared his daughter, he realized that MacKenzie looked conflicted. She was ashamed, as though she hadn't really known what was going to happen, but at the same time she was brimming with happiness at the recognition that she was getting.

"Um, yes, yes I am," Jackson said, looking back and forth be-tween the man and MacKenzie, wondering how everything had come to this.

"Well, your daughter has done a fine job for our country," the man said, seriously. "Stopping radicalized people, no matter what their relation to you is, is extremely important."

"Yes, absolutely," Jackson said, trying to mimic the man's serious tone.

He'd realized in that split second that if he didn't agree precisely with what the man said, he would instantly arouse suspicion about himself.

"We at the Bureau are incredibly proud of her," the man went on. "I'm sure the president would love to thank her personally."

The president could be the answer; Meyers could be the answer. "Uh-huh," Jackson said, looking over his shoulder at what was going on down the hall.

"If you don't come out of that room, we're going to have to bust down the door, and we'd really rather not ruin your parent's nice home," said one of the officers in front of Maya's door, his voice irritated and half amused.

"So what's going on with my other daughter?" Jackson asked, turning back to the kitchen table.

The man looked hesitant. "Well, I'm really not at liberty to tell you." He eyed Jackson's security badge in clear view hanging from his suit jacket. "But I do understand that you work with the presidential security team, so what I can say is that we will be taking your daughter with us. In fact, if I can give you some advice as a fellow professional and military man, I really think that it would be beneficial to Maya's case if you tried to talk her into surrendering peacefully."

"But, but...what did she even do?" He thought the stutter was maybe overdoing it a little, but he desperately needed to appear uninformed, as surprised as anyone else about what had happened under his roof.

The man leaned in a little, putting his elbows on the table. "Well, as you may have heard, the government is cracking down on seditious behavior. We're trying our hardest to stop smaller groups from becoming more radicalized. Thankfully, the new amendments to the National Defense Act are helping us do just that. Now that the battle with Hariq Jihad is almost done, we really need to focus on other groups that are a threat to the peace and the continued existence of our country. You may be unaware of this—in fact, in your position I'm sure that you are unaware of this, but unfortunately your daughter has fallen in with a sect of the Apocalytes, and has become increasingly radicalized about her beliefs."

"But the Apocalytes are just a sect. They're not so much terrorists, surely?" Jackson objected, trying to look shocked and disgusted.

"That's what they want you to think," the man said confidently. "But the ultimate goal of the Apocalytes, like many other groups, is to destroy the country that we have. To make it less like the great land we know and love nowadays and more like the past. Where we all lived in fear of terrorism. That is why we need to be vigilant. I know this might be rough on you, Mr. Jackson, but we really do need to take your daughter, Maya, in for her own good."

"But what will happen to her?" Jackson asked.

MacKenzie looked attentive at the question, her eyes lifting from the table top.

"As I said, I'm not at liberty to say," the man told him. "But what I can say is that everything will work out for the best."

MacKenzie looked disappointed at the lack of a real answer, and Jackson frowned. "The best?" he said. "Surely you can see why I don't think that any of this is the best situation."

"It may seem that way," the man assured him. "But eventually you'll wake up and realize that it really is for the best."

A cracking from down the hall signaled that the men had grown tired of arguing with Maya and had broken down the door.

Jackson turned. More than anything, he wanted to keep Maya from the detention centers. This was all ridiculous. He didn't have the same beliefs as his daughter, didn't think that the government was evil. He loved his country, but he couldn't see his little girl go to a detention center. He remembered that as a soldier he'd always told his men that he believed in dedication to family and country, and now he was being torn in half, being asked to choose between the two.

He almost fled to Maya's aid as two officers of the National Police Force charged into her room and physically pulled her out through the door. He couldn't give himself away, couldn't help her. The only chance of helping her that he had right now was to keep calm, keep quiet, and get to the president as soon as possible. He was the only man that Jackson thought he could turn to. His only chance.

"Come with us, ma'am," said one of the two officers.

"No," Maya said, stoically. "I refuse. Tell me what I've done wrong."

Jackson could do nothing more than watch as his daughter became a woman, standing up for what she believed in as she was physically escorted from the house. He also saw men in uniform acting the way they should, following their orders, fulfilling their duty to their country. He was saddened and torn in two because he understood both sides and was going to have to choose one.

He waited as patiently as he could as the officers loaded Maya into the truck waiting for her outside. He did all he could not to show a sign, when all he wanted was to desperately let Maya know that somehow he was going to look after her. He waited patiently as, once again, the man at the table shook hands with MacKenzie and congratulated her, and then with Jackson himself, congratulating him on raising such a fine daughter.

He waited as the men left his home, taking one of his girls away from him as his wife stood crying on the porch. Only when the neighbors lost interest and they were alone did he drag Courtney into the house and sit her at the table with MacKenzie.

"Stay here, both of you," he ordered. "Speak to no one and don't answer the phone, and definitely don't open the door. I'm going out to see what I can do."

"Daddy," said MacKenzie, looking up at him. "I'm sorry they took her away, I didn't... I thought it was right. I still think I did the right thing, but..."

Jackson put a hand on her shoulder. "It's alright, sweetie," he said. "I understand. I know. I feel the same. This is a choice so difficult that even I don't know what to decide. You just stay here with Mom and we'll talk when I get back, okay."

She nodded.

"And Court? Don't worry. It's my job to worry, and my job to look after you all."

Courtney didn't even have time to ask him where exactly he was going before Jackson was running out the front door and rushing towards his car.

The White House, Washington DC, UCSA

Jackson raced through the streets of the nation's capital. He knew that somehow he'd be able to get help from the president. Meyers was his only hope; he'd saved the damn man's life, he had to help. There was no way he'd be able to deny him. Meyers would help him get to Maya, and then he'd smuggle her out of the country. He knew that there was no way that he could convince Maya to give up her crusade. She was stubborn, just as he was, and she believed in what she believed. It would take a miracle to change her mind.

He drove faster and faster as he approached the White House, waving his security badge as he got to the booth by the parking lot, and zoomed in, screeching into his parking slot. Then he leapt from his car, running, again waving his security pass at the checkpoints, slowing to a jog but never stopping.

He didn't stop until he got to Mitzy's desk, and then gasping, he said:

"I need to see the president. Please."

She took one look at him and nodded.

"I'll slot you in, but he's with someone right now. They're just winding up, but you've gotta wait until he's done."

Jackson quickly thought on this. Interrupting the president probably wouldn't be wise. He could spare the extra couple of minutes.

"Of course," he said.

Mitzy smiled at him and nodded, and out of pure force of habit, Jackson took up his usual position in front of the oval office doors as he waited, heart thudding.

In fact, his heart was thudding so loudly that it took him a moment to realize that the president and whoever he was speaking to were standing right on the other side of the door. They must be getting ready to leave, Jackson figured. Then he realized that he could over hear every word that was being said. He didn't recognize the second voice, but from the way the conversation was going, it appeared to be someone close to the president, likely one of his rich supporters.

"Simple," Meyers was saying. "I got the order through my ear piece to move half left and then trusted my man to do the job."

"Incredible," said the other voice. "Brave and foolish, but effective."

The president laughed. "You know how to get away with assassinating the president of another country?" he asked. "Have him stand next to the President of the North American Union, that's how. All anyone cared about was whether I was okay; they never gave a thought to the fact that this was what I wanted to happen. Espinoza was never going to give me what I wanted, and I knew that Menendez would, but that he'd never have the balls to get elected. So I did what was necessary to bring me closer to my goal, closer to a United Planet, not just a United Continent. And it's cost me a fortune. That kid's family will be living in luxury for generations."

"Worth it though, I should think."

"Indeed."

Pieces fell into place and Jackson's mind whirled as he tried to show no expression. Maya was just as stubborn as him and, if it would take a miracle to change her beliefs, then the same could be said for himself. This was his epiphany and now he understood. But what the hell was he going to do? The only thing that he could, he thought, as the door opened. Save his family.

"Ah, Jackson," said Meyers, seeing him as the visitor left.

"I was wondering if I could have a quick word, sir. It's extremely important or I wouldn't be bothering you."

Meyers looked at him, noting the frantic look in Jackson's eyes, He nodded, gesturing for him to enter the room. When both were seated, Meyers raised a questioning eyebrow.

"So, what's so important then?" he asked, cheerfully.

Jackson took a deep breath. He hadn't exactly had a lot of time to think this through and he hoped to God that it worked.

"Approximately an hour ago, my oldest daughter, Maya, was arrested on charges of sedition," he began.

"I know, I know," Meyers said, waving a hand. "I thought I'd told you before that I knew everything that goes on around here."

Jackson bit his lip for a moment, then continued. "I would like to assure you that I had no knowledge of her actions whatsoever. However, of course, I am here to tender my resignation."

Meyers sat back in his chair and nodded. He watched Jackson thoughtfully for a moment before he said anything.

"You know Jackson, I didn't become president to let everything go to waste. I saw my chance, and I took it. I run this game. I realized early on that the more I could keep terrorism in the news, the more freedom I'd be given to do as I saw fit. I knew that all I needed to do was make people scared, and then I could do damn near anything so I did. Frankly, between you and I, Hariq Jihad haven't been concerned with the UCSA for years. They're far more interested in what's happening with that whole French debacle, though I've made sure that they get the weapons they need. I kept this country locked down to protect us all, and not just from terrorists. I am protecting us from ourselves. As long as people are scared, I remain president and can do as I see fit. If it benefits this country, I'll do it. If it benefits me and my ultimate goals, then I will do it immediately. As you can see, everyone that follows me is very prosperous, and those that dare oppose me, well, they find the error of their ways one way or another."

Jackson remained silent, not sure where this was heading. There were two possibilities: either he was about to be killed, so it didn't matter what the president told him, or he was being taken into the president's confidence.

"I tell you all this," the president went on, "so that you understand how seriously I take my own protection. If there had ever been even a hint of you being involved in seditious activities, you wouldn't be sitting here now. Since I take my protection so seriously, I want the best. And you are by far the best. So, in short, I do not accept your resignation. I wouldn't be here without you and your unique skills. Now that you know everything, I feel even safer with you by my side. With that being said, I want you on my full-time detail. From now on, where I go, you go."

Thank God, Jackson thought. It was what he had expected to happen, and knew that the only way that Maya's arrest wouldn't sully his reputation would be to do exactly what he'd just done. He didn't want to lose his job. If he was going to bring this system down, and that was his new goal in life, he was going to do it from the inside. It was the only way.

"Thank you, sir. It'll be my honor to be by your side." Jackson said, as humbly as he could.

"Not at all," said Meyers, with a grin. "Now, I trust that you and I have an understanding. And, of course, as long as I'm in power, you have a job, which is in your best interests obviously. Anyway, I have a meeting to get to, and you, well, I assume you need to go home and take care of your family matters. As for your daughter Maya, she is being taken for rehabilitation at a facility here in DC. I assure you she will come back to you as soon as she can."

"Yes, sir," said Jackson, standing up. "Thank you, sir."

"No problem," Meyers said.

As Jackson was leaving, there was one more thought.

"Jackson?"

"Yes?"

"I'm sorry about your daughter."

Jackson nodded and smiled in reply.

Jackson left the car on auto-drive as he tried to figure out what the hell he was going to do. He had no idea. What he did know was that, for the time being, he needed to keep his mouth shut and his nose clean. He needed to take care of Courtney and MacKenzie. He needed to figure out a way to contact Maya, tell her that he was on her side and to repent so she could be freed. Then they could work together. One thing was for damn sure: Anthony Jackson might be the president's personal security guard, entrusted with protecting the life of the leader of the UCSA, but he was also going to be the one that brought Meyers to his knees.

The car screeched as Jackson turned a corner. He was going to get his revenge, he was going to bring his country back to what it should be, and he was going to protect his family. Dedication, to his family and his true country, was all he needed to get it done, and he certainly had that. He looked out the window as the trees went by and thought to himself, "He wanted a fire war—he's going to get a fire war."

Thank you for reading Fire War. If you liked what you read please leave a review on Amazon.com and goodreads.com.

You can also contact me and/or see more about me and my books at www.firewarbooks.com

53103208R00127

Made in the USA
Charleston, SC
02 March 2016